ANGELS, WORMS, AND BOGEYS

Cascade Companions

The Christian theological tradition provides an embarrassment of riches: from Scripture to modern scholarship, we are blessed with a vast and complex theological inheritance. And yet this feast of traditional riches is too frequently inaccessible to the general reader.

The Cascade Companions series addresses the challenge by publishing books that combine academic rigor with broad appeal and readability. They aim to introduce nonspecialist readers to that vital storehouse of authors, documents, themes, histories, arguments, and movements that comprise this heritage with brief yet compelling volumes.

TITLES IN THIS SERIES:

Reading Augustine by Jason Byassee

Conflict, Community, and Honor by John H. Elliott

An Introduction to the Desert Fathers by Jason Byassee

Reading Paul by Michael J. Gorman

Theology and Culture by D. Stephen Long

Creationism and the Conflict over Evolution by Tatha Wiley

Justpeace Ethics by Jarem T. Sawatsky

Reading Bonhoeffer by Geffrey B. Kelly

FORTHCOMING TITLES:

Christianity and Politics in America by C. C. Pecknold

iPod, YouTube, Wii Play by D. Brent Laytham

Philippians in Context by Joseph H. Hellerman

Reading Revelation Responsibly by Michael J. Gorman

Angels, Worms, and Bogeys

The Christian Ethic of Pietism

Michelle A. Clifton-Soderstrom

CASCADE *Books* · Eugene, Oregon

ANGELS, WORMS, AND BOGEYS
The Christian Ethic of Pietism

Cascade Companions 11

Cascade Books
An imprint of Wipf and Stock Publishers
199 W. 8th Ave., Suite 3
Eugene, OR 97401

www.wipfandstock.com

ISBN 13: 978-1-60608-041-2

Cataloging-in-Publication data:

Clifton-Soderstrom, Michelle A.

Angels, worms, and bogeys : the Christian ethic of Pietism / Michelle A. Clifton-Soderstrom.

xii + 114 p. ; 20 cm. — Includes bibliographical references.

Cascade Companions 11

ISBN 13: 978-1-60608-041-2

1. Pietism. 2. Christian ethics. 3. Spener, Philipp Jakob, 1635–1705. 4. Petersen, Johanna Eleanora, 1644–1724. 5. Francke, August Hermann, 1663–1727. I. Title. II. Series.

BR1652 .G3 C57 2010

Manufactured in the U.S.A.

Dedication
to John, who embodies faith
to Karl, who embodies love
to Mom, who embodies hope

". . . the only thing that counts is faith working through love."
Galatians 5:6

Contents

Acknowledgments

In the course of life, there are faithful people who leave the indelible mark of Christ on your soul. To those persons who were at one time my teachers and mentors and who now are my friends and colleagues at North Park Theological Seminary, I give thanks. They formed me in various ways over the last twenty years to love Pietism. Phil, Richard, John, Jim, Paul, and the late Burton instilled in me a love for the Pietist roots of the Evangelical Covenant Church.

I acknowledge the Association of Theological Schools, Stephen Graham, and the Lilly Foundation for the Research Grant they awarded me. The opportunity to visit Halle and to work in the Pietist archives gave life to this book, and without the grant such a trip would not have been possible. The fruits of the grant remind me of the words of a widow in a letter she wrote to Francke, accompanied by the donation of her small earnings to the orphanage. God, she wrote, who can make something out of nothing, "proves it in the small and lets it be blessed."

My research was aided by the work of many. First and foremost, I am grateful to the historical work of K. James Stein, Gary Sattler, and Barbara Becker-Cantarino. Their texts on Spener, Francke, and Petersen respectively provided the much-needed foundation for my work on these Pietist figures. During our time in Halle, numerous people in the Francke Foundations and Interdisciplinary Center for Pietism Research were also helpful. In particular, I want to mention Dr. Britta Klosterberg, head of the Library, and Dr. Udo Straeter, head of the Interdisciplinary Center for Pietism Research. My conversation with Dr. Straeter revealed insights into Francke's story and the history of St. George's church. Lastly, I thank John Weborg and Gary Walter for their interviews and the insight that they offered with short notice.

I am most grateful for my students who journeyed with me in the Pietism course. They came to class prepared to sing hymns, to read Scripture together, and to discuss historical texts with great enthusiasm. For Kelly, Sarah, Jen, Paul, and David, thank you for working through the material in the early stages of my research.

My editorial work was at times overwhelming, and I am grateful for those people who aided me along the way. My sabbatical group, Kurt Peterson and Bob Hostetter, graciously read through my chapters in the eleventh hour. Max Lee helped me with New Testament translations. My husband Karl and my mother Pam read numerous drafts along the way. My teaching assistant Jamie Rose formatted my manuscript and read for clarity. Finally, one could not ask for a more professional and collegial crew than those at Wipf & Stock. I offer many thanks to all of these people.

I mention those wonderful friends who have encouraged me in multiple ways over the last year, all for whom I am continually thankful. Kerry, Phillis, Su, Max, Kurt, Cathy, Kari, Tim, and all of the children are those priestly people who pursue faith, hope and love.

Lastly, I thank Karl, who continues to be the single most inspiring person in my life. His mind greatly aids my pen, and his heart is as a good Pietist's—boundless.

Michelle A. Clifton-Soderstrom
All Saints Day, 2009

ONE

Introduction: Angels, Worms, and Bogeys

"... *the only thing that counts is faith working through love.*"
—Galatians 5:6

THE STORY BEGINS . . .

J. R. R. Tolkien's epic trilogy *The Lord of the Rings* begins modestly: "This book is largely concerned with Hobbits, and from its pages, a reader may discover much of their character and a little of their history."[1] Hobbits, in Tolkien's mythology, are a "variety" or "separate branch" of humans. From Hobbit-lore, we glean that Hobbits are hospitable and joyful, and they are good at both giving and receiving. They are also lovers of peace, adventure, and well-tilled earth.

We might describe Pietists in similar fashion, and were Hobbits real, they would likely be friends with Pietists. All humor aside, German Lutheran Pietists were in fact an odd breed, a "separate branch" of Christians, though that was never what they intended. If you were to look at a family tree of church history, you would find the Pietists branching off the Lutheran arm and extending toward the Moravians, the Free Church, Baptist General Conference, and the Evangelical

---

1. Tolkien, *Fellowship of the Ring*, 10.

1

Covenant. They have also cross-fertilized with the Reformed, Methodist, Mennonite, and even Roman Catholic branches.

This book is about the Christian ethic of Pietism. Pietism was a renewal movement that began in late seventeenth-century Germany. It was a significant movement in the Christian tradition that has been misunderstood and maligned for reasons that I will engage in the pages that follow. This book seeks to rehabilitate and understand the Pietist heritage and the central role it played in the history of Christian orthodoxy. Pietism was also vital to the origins of Evangelicalism and has much to offer Evangelicals in terms of an ethic that focuses both on Christian character and Christian practices.

While questions of when and how to mark the parameters of Pietism are quite interesting, this book is concerned with illuminating the character of the movement through the theological and social legacies of three of its earliest figures: Philipp Jacob Spener (1635–1705), August Hermann Francke (1663–1727), and Johanna Eleonora Petersen (1644–1724). These Pietists were church reformers who sought to take up the work begun by Martin Luther in the Reformation—to get back to the basic belief in the power of God's Word to engender faith and to transform human life. In the words of German theologian Jürgen Moltmann, Luther's vision can be summed as such: A reformation of life necessarily follows a reformation of faith.[2] Basing their ethic on Gal 5:6, the Pietists said it a little differently: All that matters is faith active in love.

Ironically, retrieving the basics of faith and the core of the Reformer's program made the early Pietists a minority in their Lutheran social and religious culture. They had strange

2. Moltmann, "Reformation and Revolution," 186.

theology, because they made the Bible the absolute and final authority over creedal formulations of the faith. They had unusual moral stances, because they so earnestly sought to scrutinize all of life in the light of Scripture. They were ecclesiastically disordered—they sought greater lay participation, priestly accountability, and small-group Bible studies. Though they thought themselves thoroughly Lutheran, in practice they were quite far from the Lutheran norm.

The making and shaping of Christian character was a key endeavor of the early Pietists, although they are not generally known for contributing to the history of the church in this way. Rarely do works in Pietism address questions of character and virtue. What kind of people do justice? What sort of character loves kindness? Which virtues move persons to walk humbly with their God? These questions are not the focal points of Pietist literature. And frankly, there is good reason for this gap in Pietist studies. Pietists are called individualistic, moralistic, and overly emotional. They tend toward spiritualism, mysticism, and other-worldliness. They cannot help but be, at times, rigid, separatist, and anti-intellectual. Such descriptors do not generally tempt us to raise questions of character because none of the qualities listed above qualify as a traditional virtue or excellence of character.

There are two logical reasons for the gap in studies in Christian ethics. First, Pietism is awkward, unsystematic, and difficult to define. As a movement, it splintered off quickly—making its footprint in church history both simple and complex, subtle and powerful. Moreover, they have been poorly caricatured. Reasons for this vary, but a large factor is the contentious manner that influential historical theologians, such as Albrecht Ritschl (1822–1889) and Ernst Troeltsch

(1865–1923), engaged Pietism in their writings.[3] Their critiques of Pietism included charges of extreme mysticism, separatism, and legalism—charges that still hold sway. Other notable thinkers have taken similar stances. Friedrich Engels described it in the following way:

> One only has to visit a Pietist forge or shoe repair shop. There sits the master, next to him at his right the Bible, at the left—frequently at least—the whiskey bottle. Not much work is going on. Most of the time the master reads the Bible, occasionally takes a drink, and now and then sings a hymn with his workers. Yet the main thing going on is criticizing the neighbor.[4]

The inadequate accounting exists largely because Pietism has many trajectories, and, like many movements in the history of the church, the early forms differ greatly from the later expressions. Pietism is no exception. However, as is the case for most caricatures and stereotypes, partial truth lurks somewhere in the shadows of these descriptions. Ironically, in the case of Pietism, the partial truths of these descriptors are useful and, as I shall illuminate, they actually point us to Christian character in new and fresh ways. For example, descriptions of the "other-worldly" nature of Pietism can mask the virtue that actually lies within it. Being described as other-worldly can mean that one is not aware of the realities of life on earth and therefore does not attend to its problems. This brand of other-worldliness precludes social consciousness. But a more in-depth look at a kind of other-wordliness

3. For example Ritschl, *Geschichte des Pietismus* and Treoltsch, *The Social Teachings of the Christian Churches*.

4. Herzog, *European Pietism Reviewed*, 1.

that is embedded in a deep sense of hope reveals a virtue that paradoxically inspired the Pietist movement not only to develop their social consciousness but to *respond* to social ills. Such examples point to the fact that while Pietism may be unsystematic and unwieldy, their Christian ethic is full of theologically innovative and ethically rich practices.

The second possibility for the gap in Pietist ethics is the inability to imagine how intense readers of Scripture could also engage in moral activism. The Pietists were known for spending much time gathered around the Word. Moreover, their writings chronicled their experiences of conversion and new life in Christ—not the ways they were socially active. The writings that did concern ethics seemed rule-based, such as some of Francke's work. There also exist biases against the social reaches of Pietism. These biases are due, in part, to Pietism's Lutheran theological commitments and the perception that Luther's two-kingdom doctrine—that separated the spiritual kingdom of love from the earthly kingdom of the sword or politics—had no real integrated Christian social ethic. Nevertheless, I will show in the pages that follow that the Lutheranism operative in Pietism along with the Pietist emphasis on faith, hope, and love directly counter negative presuppositions about the moral contours of Pietist theology. Moreover, the primary avenue for understanding the subtle moral contours of Pietism requires us to connect their theological commitments to the witness of their characters.

In recent years, German scholars and church historians have done far superior work in studying Pietism. This book supports and engages the clarifying historical work of such American church scholars as Gary Sattler, K. James Stein, Dale Brown, and Jonathan Strom in celebrating the many contributions of Pietism. In addition, this book continues the theological trajectories of theologian C. John Weborg. In a significant article on Pietism and the Christian vocation, he writes of some of the treasures of the Pietist's understanding of doctrine and life.[5] In sum, he concludes that for the Pietists, doctrine and life are inseparable. Doctrine is meant to give life—it is to be embodied in Christian living and give shape to our identity. On the flip side, Christian life-practices frame the ways that we talk about God. For example, the practice of reading Scripture with the aid of the Holy Spirit offers faithful people rich insights into such doctrinal questions as: Who is God? Who are we? What is the Trinity? What does it mean to take baptismal vows? What happens when we die? Why celebrate the Lord's Supper? Further, the explanation of these questions shapes how we then care for one another in the face of death or how we offer hospitality to others through food.

The neglect of Pietist ethics is not merely a gap in the scholarly literature. More importantly, the neglect is a gap in the story of the Christian people. Why read the about Pietist ethics? For this one simple reason: they represent a faithful account of rigorous Christianity, and Christian ethics is fundamentally about rigorous Christianity. Pietist ethics are accessible to all branches of the church, in large part because the life of the movement lies in their commitment to the church's common source—the Word of God as it engenders the response of faith, hope, and love. This one simple thing makes the Pietists worth reading about.

---

5. Weborg, "Pietism: A Question of Meaning and Vocation."

Angels, Worms, and Bogeys?

"Angels, Worms, and Bogeys" playfully frames key aspects of Pietists ethics—but not as analogies. The trilogy is not exactly "faith, hope, and love," but, strangely, angels, worms, and bogeys offer insight into the three theological virtues because they show how Pietism has been interpreted and what Pietism has to offer. The first two, angels and worms, refer to Gary Sattler's book on Pietist anthropology—their understanding of the nature of human beings.[6] In his book, Sattler notes the movements in the history of Christianity that have placed major attention on human beings' relationship to God. The idea of Christ living in the individual is the core of the Christian faith, and this shift re-situates the function of creeds and doctrines as the only way to know God. Pietism, which grew out of Lutheranism, was an example of a movement that valued a personal relationship with God. Sattler notes that for movements such as these, "God-talk and anthropology are inseparable."[7] The focus on the human condition in relation to the Creator fostered a preoccupation with sin, and drove Pietists such as August Hermann Francke to designate human beings as "nothing but, or . . . even lower than, a worm."[8] Likening human beings to worms marked the depths of the human condition in relation to God.

Beyond Sattler's work and Francke's designation, I chose worms because they represent the depths of Pietism in our historiography. Pietists loved biological metaphors for describing the Christian life. Those familiar with Pietism might

---

6. Sattler, *Nobler than the Angels.*

7. Ibid., ix.

8. Ibid., xi.

enjoy retaining the designation "worms" because it describes their attentiveness to their environment well. Pietists are like worms not only because they had the courage to confront the effects of sin in human beings but also because they were able to transform the environment of the church. By digesting God's Word and allowing it to penetrate their lives, Pietism revived dead dirt and turned it into living soil. The soil they helped create became the environment from which social engagement, lay participation, and missionary activity increased. The soil they renewed helped grow the priesthood to be a body deeply grounded in a life-giving faith.

Angels, on the other hand, signify the heights to which humans can aspire when they are born anew. According to Sattler, the flip side of Pietist anthropology is that when we envision the soul as it was created to be, namely renewed in God's image, we have a window into the true nobility of humans.[9] This nobility is higher even than the angels, and we experience it when we are continually transformed and regenerated by the power of the Holy Spirit. While tendencies toward perfectionism existed in some aspects of Pietism, they were merely tendencies. Pietists were not really perfectionists. They were interested in human flourishing as it came about in the context of God's intention in creation. New birth and new life in Christ was God's intention for creation and, hence, the most good and noble portrayal of human beings.

I also chose angels because they represent the heights of Pietism in our historiography. Pietism affirmed the loftiest aspects of the Christian faith. They did not simply talk about the excellences of faith, love, and hope—they lived faithfully,

9. Ibid., 32.

lovingly, and hopefully. My colleague, C. John Weborg, often walks our students through the Great Thanksgiving. When he gets to the point when we proclaim the mystery of faith—Christ has died! Christ is risen! Christ will come again!—he stops. The room is silent. Head bent humbly, all the while looking his students straight in the eye, John asks, "Now, do you believe it?" Christians recite many things in a given day, week or month. The question is whether we believe what we say and we say what we believe. The Pietists sought to bring these together in ways that had lofty expectations and mystical qualities. In this way, they remind us of the angels. They are like angels in that they strove to mediate that which was heavenly.

And then we have bogeys. In a footnote in *The Politics of Jesus*, John Howard Yoder takes on historians and theologians who use the term "pietistic" to describe movements that have spiritualized Christian ethics.[10] He contends that such epithetical use of the term "pietistic" is bogus because it diminishes the creative and critical contributions of the actual historical movement that was Pietism. Yoder, and others such as Dale Brown,[11] refer to the bogey of Pietism in order to identify its positive contributions. Bogeys cause confusion and trouble. In golf, a bogey is one over par, below average, and less than expected. Such has been the picture of Pietism—that it is a movement that has hurt the history of the Christian church more than it has advanced it and that its Christian ethic is sub-par—a bogey rather than an eagle, to stick with the golf metaphor.

10. Yoder, *Politics of Jesus*, 22. Yoder also takes this up in *Christian Witness to the State*, 84.

11. Brown, "Bogey of Pietism."

If worms and angels mark the heights and depths of Pietism and perhaps the clearest aspects of the character of the movement, the "bogey" marks everything in-between. It marks, as we will see in the conclusion, the places where faith, love, and hope come together. It marks where God meets us and we respond. In some of the less-than-adequate, bogus views of the faithful and challenging aspects of Pietism, we indeed find much evidence of God at work. And so, the term bogey is a way to approach the confusing aspects of Pietism in order to get at the nature and character of their Christian ethic. Pietism has caused trouble. Nevertheless, its trouble is worth redeeming.

CLARIFYING THE BOGEY

So, what do we mean by the term Pietism? In 1689, Leipzig poet Joachim Feller wrote a poem describing Pietism, and one verse reads:

> Pietists—the name is now well-known throughout
> the world. What is a Pietist? One who studies God's
> Word. And also leads a holy life according to it. . .
> Piety must first of all nest in the heart.[12]

This poem is notably one of the first formal attempts to define a Pietist. While Spener originally thought the term derogatory and too sectarian, in the end its use became acceptable because it did connect with Pietism's primary traits—studying God's Word, a faith of the heart, and a connection between faith and life.

---

12. Beyreuther, *August Hermann Francke*, 67.

Pietism was at root a renewal movement that began in the devastating wake of the Thirty Years' War. Beyond that, historians' views of the movement differ based on how they define the historical parameters and how they construct the theological web that connects the origins with some of the separatist tendencies. Some views have strict historical parameters. Others, due to Pietism's broad tentacles, view it as a renewal movement that still exists today. While I acknowledge and affirm Pietism's wide historical application, for the purposes of this book, I use what is called the constructionist model, supported by historians such as Johannes Wallman. It dates Pietism beginning with Philipp Jakob Spener in the late seventeenth century and moves through the Pietist activity in the eighteenth century, including its cross-fertilization with other movements. The view I take includes August Hermann Francke as a primary figure of Halle Pietism and also designates other centers of Pietism around Germany, such as Württemberg. This framing of the movement is most clearly bound historically and allows for greater ease in characterizing Pietism and its origins in their specificity.

The unifying theological characteristics of Pietism included an emphasis on the individual's relationship with God, a devotion to Scripture, and a strong understanding of the sanctifying work of the Holy Spirit in the life of the believer. Further, they shared a love for preaching and for the sacramental life of the church. The Pietist's focus on church renewal was a response to the strict confessionalism and clericalism in the orthodox Lutheran church as well as an attempt to work out some of the unresolved issues of the Reformation. The Pietists sought to return to Luther's emphasis on a living faith, the power of the Word, and a strong common priesthood.

These last three, in particular, occupied much of Pietist life
and thought because they were concerned with the ministry
of the whole church. Faith and Scripture were two essential
elements of a strong common priesthood. While they have
often been seen as weakening the office of ordination, the
Pietists were in actuality concerned with strengthening the
priesthood in order to also strengthen the office of ordination. This was not a move for more power. Rather, it was an
effort to have a more mutually functioning body that was
well formed in the Word of God and that could minister to
the world. They believed that the spiritual functions of the
priesthood, including alms, prayer, sacrifice, admonishment,
and holding the pastor accountable, were open to all. The ordained clergy were to be the guides and leaders forming all
Christians for the spiritual activity of the church. The aim of
a strong priesthood was both an expanded priesthood in the
church and a greater evangelical witness to the world.

Because of their theological emphases and the cultivation of practices such as gathering in small groups to read
Scripture together and empowering the laity, tendencies
toward sectarianism and individualism existed. This moved
some of the more zealous Pietist communities into what is
known as Radical Pietism—the other primary branch of
German Pietism tending toward extremism and separation
from the established church.[13] I should note that historians
often place my third figure—Johanna Eleanora Petersen—in
the radical branch of Pietism. However, she was deeply
formed by Spener and a friend of both Spener and Francke,
consulting them both throughout her life. While the genre of

---

13. For more on Radical Pietism, see Schneider, *German Radical
Pietism*.

her writing falls within the style of the more mystical qualities of Radical Pietism, the content of her work nests well on the Spener-Francke branch of the movement. The interpretation of her writing and her placement in the radical arena carries some gender biases with it, and I will address these more fully in chapter 3.

Ecclesially, Pietism had strong roots not only in Lutheranism but also in the Reformed tradition, particularly in Puritanism. It also had connections with medieval mysticism, Quakers, Jansenists, Anabaptists, Baptists, Moravians, Methodists, and other holiness movements. This book focuses on their primary context, the Lutheran Church in Germany, as it marks the unifying theological characteristics of other ecclesial manifestations of Pietism. Further, the German Pietists represent the early center of the movement making a widespread familiarity with this aspect of the movement all the more important for Evangelicals.

Within German Lutheran Pietism, a few distinctions stand out. First, they were ecclesially minded. Though there was emphasis on the individual's conversion and experience of faith, they had a high view of the church and valued participation in the community of faith through worship and devotion. Second, they were politically and socially involved. They were innovative educational reformers, incorporating education with social mindedness. They influenced political changes in early modern Europe, including the transformation of Prussia.[14] Third, they were globally minded. They had a passion for evangelism and missions, and they communi-

14. For more on the Pietist influence in Prussia, particularly through the friendship of Francke and King Frederick William I, see Gawthrop, *Pietism and the Making of Eighteenth Century Prussia*.

cated widely with areas of the world such as India, Russia, England, North America, and the larger Atlantic World.[15]

As I use the term Pietism throughout this companion, the reader can assume that I am referring to German Lutheran Pietism, and in particular Halle Pietism. I will indicate when I diverge from this usage. Moreover when I discuss doctrines such as regeneration, or new life in Christ, or when I reflect on practices such as conventicles, or reading Scripture, the reader can also assume that I am situating these specifically within the German Lutheran Pietist context.

REDEEMING THE BOGEY

My primary goal in this book is to help my readers discover the beauty of Pietist ethics. In the scope of Christian ethics, there are a variety of paradigms that describe the task of theological ethics as well as the kinds of questions that Christians raise and ways Christians go about answering those questions. Some approaches emphasize the decisions that we make in life. Should I live in a diverse neighborhood? Should I consider in-vitro fertilization? Should I learn a second language? Vote for a Democrat or Republican? Vote at all? These kinds of questions lead to judgments using principles such as rules, laws, or rights that are informed by a variety of authorities including Scripture. Such approaches are decision-based. They value right decisions as they align with specific principles. The actions that follow constitute the central aspect of what it means to live faithfully.

---

15. For more on this, see Strom, Lehman, and Melton, *Pietism in Germany and North America.*

Virtue approaches to ethics, on the other hand, focus on the character of a person or a community. A virtue is an excellence of character that is developed over time through habit. Excellences of character are determined by the nature of the thing or being, and they predispose something to be and do what it was meant to be and do. For example, part of what it means to be a boat is to float, and so buoyancy is an excellence, or virtue, of a good boat. Buoyancy enables the boat to do an important aspect of what it was created to do, namely float.

Virtues are determined, then, by figuring out who or what we are, and they equip us by enabling us to act well in light of this identity. Because identity is so important in virtue ethics, stories and narratives are critical vehicles in discerning character excellences that communities seek to cultivate. In virtue ethics, the onus is on the community to interpret or navigate the story well because embedded stories determine excellences and, further, offer rituals and ways to habituate persons to become excellent or virtuous. Traditionally, the Christian church has noted seven core virtues. These include the four cardinal virtues—or virtues from which others emerge: prudence, justice, temperance and courage. They also include the three theological virtues: faith, hope and love. These emerge from the context of Scripture (i.e., Rom 5:1–5; 1 Cor 13:13; Col 1:4–5) and the practices of the historical church.

At a cursory glance, attempts to characterize Pietist ethics might tend toward the former decision-based approach. Pietists paid detailed attention to personal conduct and moral norms. Philipp Jakob Spener was known to have rejected all "worldly vanity" and from an early age to have led an earnestly pious and moral life. Johanna Eleonora Petersen wrote about her conscious rejection of non-edifying activities such as dancing and drinking. And August Hermann Francke, who oversaw hundreds of children, developed numerous sets of lists and rules and was known to be somewhat moralistic about instituting them. It is not surprising that writers of history have equated Pietism with moralism given some of the above examples.

Yet, as I will show in the succeeding chapters, this is only the surface of the story. At the heart of Pietist ethics are a practice-centered ethic that finds its source in the formation of Christian character. I interpret Pietism through a character-, or virtue-based lens because of the way in which the theological virtues function in their theology and practices. C. John Weborg calls this phenomenon "the convergence of Pietism."[16] While the convergence in Pietism centers on the joining of doctrine and life, the phenomenon also exists in the realm of the theological virtues. The manner in which the Pietists delved into the biblical narrative deeply connected with their practices of faith, hope, and love in their distinct Christian contours.

The convergence in the theological virtues as they are embodied in the Pietists gets at the heart of how they viewed Christian ethics as living lives that pointed to the gospel. While all of the pieces of justice, compassion, mercy, and evangelism are present, none of these constituted the end of the ethical life. The purpose of the ethical life was to live as we were created to be—as created by God. As such, our lives are to be portraits of the living God, portraits of the gospel of Jesus Christ. In a sense, the ethical life was about giving

16. Weborg, "Pietism: A Question of Meaning and Vocation."

everything back to God. The beauty of their Christian ethic was that they enacted justice, compassion, mercy, and evangelism along the way. Because their witness to the gospel was the only end of the Christian life, they powerfully embodied an ethic that relied on the theological virtues—on the excellences that Christians receive from God and cultivate over time through habit. These virtues—faith, hope, and love—simply and powerfully defined what it meant for Pietists to be the people of God.

The mechanics of theological virtues is wonderfully embodied in the Pietists, and differs slightly from the manner that other virtues are cultivated and achieved. In the previous examples of the boat and of the cardinal virtues, we can note their respective excellences (e.g., buoyancy and wisdom respectively), and then we can imagine their corresponding actions (e.g., floating and discerning respectively). However, in the theological virtues, the excellence and corresponding action are one and the same. As do doctrine and life, the theological virtues converge. I use the biblical Greek to highlight the mechanics of the theological virtues as their noun (excellence) and verbal (action) forms converge. The meaning of faith is trust or belief. The excellence of faith (*pistis*) is also the action of faith (*pisteuō*)—I have belief and I believe. The excellence of hope (*elpis*) is also the action of hope (*elpizō*)—I have hope and I hope. And finally, the excellence of love (*agapē*) is also the action of love (*agapaō*)—I have love and I love. This is the unique quality of the theological virtues. It is a uniqueness that is particularly evident in the Pietists and their Christian ethic, and illuminating these convergences in the character of the early figures and the origins of their history is what I call redeeming the bogey.

MUCH CHARACTER AND A LITTLE HISTORY . . .

The chapters of this book are organized around two sets of threes. The first are the three figures—Philipp Jacob Spener, August Hermannn Francke, and Johanna Eleonora Petersen. I chose them for a variety of reasons. Philipp Jacob Spener was considered the father of German Lutheran Pietism, and he authored the movement's seminal text, *Pia Desideria*—or *Heartfelt Desire for a God-Pleasing Reform of the True Evangelical Church, Together with Several Simple Proposals Looking Toward This End*. He began conventicles, the small-group reading of Scripture, and these gatherings became one of the defining practices of Pietism. He was a theologian and a pastor. His primary concern was a renewed church, and his book, the *Pia*, spelled out a practical program for renewing the church of his day.

If Spener was the thinker of the Pietist movement, August Hermannn Francke was the activist. Situated in Halle-Glaucha—a German city near Leipzig—Francke worked as a seminary professor, devoted scholar, and pastor. His parish of St. George's was located in the impoverished area of town, Glaucha. During his ministry there, Francke became impassioned about the situation of the underprivileged and poor. An astute pastor like his mentor Spener, Francke knew the needs of his flock very well, and most of them were basic—food, clothing, shelter, and an education. In effort to meet these needs, Francke was able to weave social reform that encompassed developing orphanages, schools, poor houses, and homes for widows and beggars into his desires for Christian formation. In doing so, he altered the social conditions not only of Glaucha and Halle, but also of the Prussian state through his influence on Fredrick William I.

While Spener and Francke were well-known leaders of the Pietist movement, Johanna Eleonora Petersen was lesser known, perhaps because she was a woman and a lay person. Petersen was a parishioner of Spener's and a friend to both Spener and Francke. Her Christian excellence showed up in her devotion to God in conjunction with her relationships with people, as a teacher, leader, friend, theologian, and sometimes preacher. She inserted her faith into all aspects of life. Her passion lay in the promise that faith makes us new creatures in Christ, and she taught, wrote, and lived with evangelistic fervor. She wrote and published many works, including her own spiritual autobiography. A woman who used her gifts creatively, Petersen modeled numerous ways women could participate in church leadership, and, furthermore, she pushed social boundaries that inhibited women's roles in public life.[17]

I also chose Spener, Francke, and Petersen because, as important as their individual achievements were, they also exemplified the spiritual priesthood working together as one body. These three figures were not ecclesial cowboys who saved the day by themselves. They worked together—they befriended one another, formed one another, and supported one another. Spener appointed Francke to his positions in Halle. Francke made some of Spener's theology of church renewal come to life. Petersen was an active lay member in Spener's church and corresponded with Francke, offering words of

17. Recent scholarship in Pietism and in women's studies, including Barbara Becker-Cantarino's translation of Petersen's autobiography, is surging, as are studies in the area of the role of spiritual autobiography in eighteenth-century German Pietism. Other sources include Martin, "Female Reformers as the Gatekeepers of Pietism" and Weisner, *Gender, Church, and State in Early Modern Germany*.

encouragement. In some ways, they were ordinary Christians who used their gifts well and who engaged basic practices on a daily basis. In other ways, they were extraordinary because through their faithful practices they were co-participants in renewing the church and in expanding the priesthood to include marginalized people. In the end, their devotion to Christ and practices of faith reveal that these categories—ordinary and extraordinary—collapse when one engages the gospel faithfully and when the common priesthood works together on behalf of the church's mission.

The second set of three are the questions that focus the following three chapters and that correspond with each of the three figures. In his scriptural rules of life, Francke called for Christians to remember three things—to believe what Scripture teaches, do what Scripture commands, and hope what Scripture promises. His approach to Scripture was to ask how we ought to believe, live, and hope. In light of Francke's approach, each chapter corresponds with one of Francke's questions, namely: How should we believe? How should we live? And, how should we hope?

The first, How should we believe?, deals with the virtue of faith and aspects of Christian doctrine. It explores and engages the central claims about God, the ways that their theology was both orthodox and life-giving, and the methods that served Pietist thought about who God is—always in relation to human beings. Baptism and conversion were key experiences, and the doctrinal focus of the Pietists reflected these in their understanding of regeneration. Regeneration encompassed the relationship between justification—God's justifying work in Christ on the cross—and sanctification—the ongoing work of new life generated in the Christian through the work of the Holy Spirit. Faith includes, then, both receiving it as a gift and cultivating it through habits.

The figure-focus in this chapter is Spener. In telling Spener's story, I make use of the great gift that Spener left the church—the *Pia Desideria*. The *Pia* offers a comprehensive proposal for the renewing the church. An underlying assumption of the text is that the ministry of the church cannot accomplish all that it ought without the help of the whole spiritual priesthood. Analogous to the converted Christian as the recipient of faith in the form of ongoing regeneration, a converted priesthood is the recipient faith in the form of ongoing ecclesial renewal. Faith in both its individual and communal forms bears fruit. This fruit was seen in their character and in the way that the priesthood worked together. In the case of Spener, his faithful work with his parish practically extended the common priesthood, breaking through such sinful barriers as class to include the poor in the common priesthood.

The second question, How should we live?, deals with ways Christians bring together love of God and love of neighbor. I examine practices that capture the depth of incorporating the Word of God and the act of the Holy Spirit in the life of the Christian—acts such as spiritual autobiography and letter writing as they frame how we understand the double command to love. In this chapter, the narrative focus is on Petersen as she exemplified these practices in creative ways. Her growth and formation as a female servant of Christ serve as an inspiration to the whole church, including laity, teachers and clergy.

The question, How should we live?, frames the theological virtue of love as it is nourished through Christian practices. The chapter assumes that Christian love is something that faithful people work diligently to acquire. It acts upon faith and infiltrates the ordinary and mundane. As Petersen showed, love helps Christians endure one another and forgive one another. Petersen's life and writings demonstrated the Pietist's motto of faith acting in love. Like Spener, she worked together with the priesthood and in doing so broke through sinful barriers such as gender and encouraged the priesthood to embrace the gifts of women.

The third question, How should we hope?, examines the larger social effects of the church working in the world. Hope marks the drive in the equation *faith acting in love*. Hope constitutes the acting piece, because it is in hope that one enacts the vision of faith and love that is presented in the gospel, as Paul writes in Colossians (1:4–5). Hope is the activity by which one's life points beyond itself to the heavenly.

Francke is the focus of this chapter, and his social reforms in Germany point us, quite literally, to the heavenly. When I began writing this book, I started with the chapter on hope because hope is the excellence through which Pietism demonstrated the power of the Christian witness. Hope is the lifeblood of Christian ethics, and all of the Pietists had it. However, it finds particular fruition in the life and work of Francke. Through his reforms, Francke too worked diligently to extend the common priesthood. In his case, the common priesthood broke the barriers of age and reached out to include the children.

FINALLY, WHO SHOULD READ THIS BOOK?

Pietism is one of the least understood movements in the history of the church, and so this book informs and explains. It explores the ethical and theological commitments that carved out the movement's place in the history of the church. Pietism is also one of the most influential Protestant movements since the Reformation. Hence, this book celebrates a movement of intensely faithful people. These people were largely lay people who were committed to their ecclesial communities as well as their neighborhoods. They understood reform as a function of basic Christian practices. Reading Scripture in groups, for example, invokes the Holy Spirit's work of love in the world. And, herein lies the practical significance of this book: the retrieval of simple Christian practices as they witness to the gospel of Jesus Christ. In a world that is immensely bound by schedules, busyness, virtual relationships, global mobility, technology, and access to everything under the sun, I write to remind Christians that the gospel calls us to some fairly basic practices. We are so easily overwhelmed by trying to fix this messy world, that we forget that salvation is not our job but God's. We are called to live faithfully and to allow God to work through us, the church. In writing about these reformers, my intent is, like theirs, to witness to the gospel through the lives of the faithful so that others may grow in their own faith in Christ and so that through belief, we might have life in his name.

This book is primarily for Evangelicals who want an accessible book that shows the theological and ethical character of a movement that greatly influenced the Evangelical Church in North America. Pietist hymnody can be found in the hymnals of all major American denominations.[18] Pietists affected the spirit of evangelical preaching. They contributed significantly to devotional literature as well as impacted the social outreach of the Church.[19] The movement arguably produced such great figures as Walter Rauschenbusch and Billy Graham.[20] They had influence on the Wesleys and the Methodist church, the baptists, and, of course, the Lutheran and Reformed churches. They played a formative role in the Moravian leader and bishop Count Nicolaus Ludwig von Zinzendorf. They initiated the earliest missions in India and had relationships in Russia. They were, at root, a renewal movement that influenced and energized the Great Awakenings in both England and North America. Finally, they contributed much in the way of educational reform in the eighteenth century.

It is important for Evangelicals to be familiar with their historical roots and the character of those who helped shape their identity. The Evangelical church in the United States is in a period of uncertainty, lacking in a unified identity. We are split in the areas of social issues, politics, worship, and theology. Whether Evangelicals will ever have a unified identity is uncertain, but a minimal step in this direction includes a willingness to retrieve and reincorporate our roots—to re-engage, in a sense, our family heritage. In the case of retrieving Pietism, an example might include acknowledging the power of the Word of God not just in theory but in practice. So, for

18. Religious studies professor Ernst Stoeffler wonders where American hymnody would be without the hymns that were Pietistic in origin. See Stoeffler, *Rise of Evangelical Pietism*, 3.

19. Ibid., 4.

20. Brown, "Bogey of Pietism," 12–18.

example, we know our Bibles by reading them regularly—not just parts, but all of it. One result might be that the whole of Scripture then grounds our moral conversation in far richer ways than political platitudes, uniting us more deeply in the faith and overcoming some of the political divisions within current Evangelicalism.

If we were to ask, So what? Why not just write a book on reading Scripture?, Evangelicals would agree with that. Why bring in the Pietists? My simple answer is that Evangelicals need a voice outside the current moment in history to ground them. In times of identity crises, internal tension, conflict over where the church's energies should focus—in those moments, we would do well to remember that there is a whole history of Christian communities that could serve as our outside voices, our external critics, our cloud of support and encouragement. In the Pietist movement that so greatly influenced the birth of Evangelicalism, we find that outside voice calling us back to the basics of Christian living in ever-deepening ways along with the support that comes from the very character of their commitment to edifying the whole body. It is time for Evangelicals to better know their Bibles—always, but it is also time for Evangelicals to better know their history and learn from their Christian exemplars.

This book is also for my own denomination, the Evangelical Covenant Church. We are a church who emerged from rural, impoverished areas of Sweden and whose early life was shaped by Swedish immigrants who came to North America. Our constitution names our two greatest historical influences as Swedish Lutheranism and Pietism. The increasing growth and diversity in our denomination is largely due to the values of our Pietist foremothers and forefathers, and their commitment to compassion, justice, and mercy as they witness to the gospel. These are the makings of a faithful church, and it is for my Evangelical Covenant sisters and brothers that I write the Pietist story enthusiastically.

This companion is essentially a museum book. It beckons, "Come, reader, and let us re-imagine the contribution of the seventeenth-eighteenth century movement in Germany called Pietism. Really, this will be fun and the book should engage you holistically."

In an attempt to be holistic himself, Francke created a room in the school that he called the "Cabinet of Artifacts and Curiosities." In this room, he collected artifacts and gems from all around the world for his students to hold and ponder. Francke acted as a sort of curator of cultural and natural treasures evoking the children to move from curiosity to wonder. Pietists, like some cultural artifacts, are curious people, most certainly, but they warrant more than a glance or a single visit. It is my hope that like Francke, I can be the kind of curator who facilitates my readers to move from curiosity to wonder, leaving you with a sense of the beauty portrayed by the faith, hope, and love of the early Pietists.

TWO

How Should We Believe?

"Faith makes us an altogether changed people."
—Philipp Jakob Spener

Philipp Jakob Spener was born converted. Or, at least, he never claimed to remember a moment when he did not know Christ. Spener was nurtured in faith from birth. At the young age of five days old, he was baptized into the care of the church. They declared him as one of God's children and, as history would show, these faithful people followed through on their vow to nurture him in the Christian faith. Spener's parents were pious people in the Lutheran tradition. They housed a library with many theological books in German and in English that they encouraged Spener to read. Spener was also blessed with an involved godmother, the Countess Agathe of Rappoldstein. Countess Agathe loved children and taught them well. She energetically cared for the young Philipp as she did for her own stepchildren and other local children.[1] An educated woman, Countess Agathe spent time with Spener, forming him in the faith, instructing and admonishing him in a loving spirit. Spener was only thirteen when she died, and before her death she paid for his entrance into

1. For more, see Stein, *Philipp Jakob Spener*, 36ff.

the university, securing the future of his education. Countess Agathe took her baptismal vows seriously—and they paid off. While Spener would go on to have many mentors, Countess Agathe was one of Spener's earliest priests.

Like his godmother, Spener lived baptismally. He trusted both God and his brothers and sisters in Christ. He had much hope that the church was the body called to nurture and form one another in faith. Spener's faith that God worked through the church was tested early in his vocational life when he was called to two ministerial positions. The first call was from Spener's home town of Strasburg. He wanted this position, and he was at home in the Strasburg parish. However, the Lutheran church in Frankfurt also wanted to appoint Spener as their senior clergy person. The Frankfurt position intimidated Spener because it included overseeing other ministers far senior in both age and experience to Spener's own thirty-one years. He left the decision for the churches to decide between themselves, although he indicated his own thoughts on the matter. In the end, Strasburg decided to send Spener to Frankfurt, and so Spener went and took up his new responsibilities. Though he took this post with trepidation, he firmly believed that God had spoken clearly through his church.

Spener's answer to the question, "How should we believe?," has a short version and a long one. The short is: Believe by putting your baptism into constant use throughout your life! Inasmuch as baptism is an identity marker, it is serious, everyday business. The orthodox Lutheran view of baptism was that it was regenerative in the once and for all, salvific sense. Spener, however, thought this truncated the ongoing role of baptism in the life of the Christian and, furthermore, the rich ecclesial context of baptism. His hope was that persons would not forget their baptism, because he wanted persons to embrace their faith. He agreed with his Lutheran colleagues that baptism was a once and for all sacrament because Christ's one death was sufficient. However, baptism also functioned as a lifelong birthmark designating persons' membership into a new kingdom—the kingdom that Jesus began in his ministry of reconciliation, his death, and his resurrection. The resurrection of Christ directs the reality of this new kingdom. Baptism into it impresses on us, Spener believed, particularly as we grow by using our identity in ways not unlike persons grow into and utilize the gifts and responsibilities that accompany other kinds of membership, such as national citizenship. As members of God's kingdom, our baptismal identity strengthens and grows as we remember who we are and act accordingly. The gift of faith that goes along with this membership benefits us—but we have to *receive* faith and *use* faith. Spener understood baptism as an ongoing regenerative power in the life of the individual and the church when it was accompanied by an active faith. Because baptism in his day was synonymous with national citizenship and therefore not taken seriously, Spener felt the need to uplift it in ways fitting to the reality of God's grace as it beckons us: ". . . if your baptism is to benefit you, it must remain in constant use throughout your life."[2] This, in fact, is how we should believe—by using our baptism and by growing more deeply in our vows to love and form one another.

The long version of the answer to, "How should we believe?," is rooted in the ways Spener's pastoral ministry sought to cultivate the excellence of faith. Toward the end

---

2. Spener, *Pia Desideria*, 66.

of his twenty years of ministry in Frankfurt, Spener wrote the seminal Pietist text *Pia Desideria*. The *Pia* consisted of six simple proposals for the renewal of faith in the life of the church. These included:

1. More extensive use of the Word of God.
2. The establishment and exercise of the spiritual priesthood.
3. Christianity that consists of the practice of faith not just knowledge of the faith.
4. Good conduct in religious controversies.
5. Excellent seminary training and formation.
6. Preaching for the purpose of edification.

The aim of these proposals was the cultivation of a vital, regenerative faith, and Spener believed that these could be grown with apposite ministerial routines that challenged and facilitated faith. Spener sought to embody his program in the *Pia* and to engender a stronger, more faithful, priesthood through four ministerial practices. These four practices included catechism, conventicles, the sacramental life, and preaching. While other ministerial practices facilitated the faith of the priesthood, to be sure, these four were distinctive elements of Spener's pastoral ministry and stemmed from his strong views on baptism as an ongoing regenerative power in the life of the church. Before turning to these practices as the long version of the answer to How should we believe?, let us look at Spener's understanding of regeneration as it gave context to his ministerial practices.

THE SERIOUS BUSINESS OF BAPTISM: REGENERATION

The Pietists loved organic metaphors to describe the Christian life, and regeneration was a primary example. If Luther thought that the doctrine of justification was the article by which the church stands or falls, the analogous Pietist conviction would be that the doctrine of regeneration was the doctrine by which the church lives or dies. Regeneration refers to the unity of two things in the life of the believer: the justifying work of Christ and sanctifying work of the Holy Spirit. In biological terms, regeneration is the Holy Spirit planting seeds in Christians that bear fruits of faith. In the New Testament, the term "regeneration" occurs in Titus 3:5 in the context of the waters of rebirth and renewal. This is one of two places in the New Testament that uses regeneration, and it significantly occurs as a trajectory of new life (the fruit born by the one who accepts faith) that emerges from new birth (the seed planted by the Holy Spirit).

Regeneration encompasses the major points of God's saving activity—what I call the theological "news": new birth, new life, new creation, new heavens, and new earth. If we were to pick up a text in systematic theology, we probably would not find a chapter devoted to the doctrine of regeneration. Rather, we might find the doctrines that regeneration encompasses, including baptism and conversion, sin and salvation, faith and works, and justification and sanctification. Regeneration is operative in baptism as we die with Christ and receive forgiveness for our sins. Regeneration is operative in faith as we become new creations by being born again. Regeneration is operative in the new heavens and new earth as we look toward the new kingdom that Jesus began.

The encompassing newness of regeneration in light of God's saving story emerges in what Spener described as a three-fold movement. Firstly, God ignites faith in one's heart or what Spener would also have called the human will. While we human beings can resist grace, we cannot bring about this extension and offer of grace. Both the capacity to resist God and the inability to initiate faith are the effects of sin. When we accept God's offer of grace, God enables us to believe and enlivens our faith as we hear the Word. God's Word is operative, and Spener referred to God's words in Scripture as a "heavenly light" and a "power at work."[3]

Secondly, new birth, which is initially given in baptism, becomes the basis for justification. Baptism is not regenerative in the sense that it *causes* salvation; however, it does participate in God's saving work.[4] Paul points to this in Titus 3 in celebrating God's saving work through the water of rebirth. Newborn persons have their sins forgiven. They are justified and adopted as God's children. Further, they are initiated through baptism into priestly service.[5]

Thirdly, the work of the Holy Spirit creates an entirely new person—a new spirit which permeates one's whole being. In this third movement of regeneration, we perceive ourselves

3. Stein, *Philipp Jakob Spener*, 190.

4. As an aside, Spener would never say that anything we do causes salvation. Soteriology is completely the power of God, and we are merely participants in it.

5. Spener wrote an entire catechism on the subject of the priesthood of believers. In it, he shows baptism not only to be an adoption into the body of Christ but also into priestly service. This is based on the Old Testament view of being born into the tribe of Levi as a birth into priestly service. For more, see Weborg, *Eschatological Ethics of Johann Albrecht Bengel*, 10.

as constantly standing in God's presence. We have a thirst for God's Word, a power to pray in the Spirit, a grace-inspired patience in suffering, and finally, a deep sense of hope. This new nature is our inner impulse toward God. It is neither perfect nor without struggle, yet it is, in Spener's words, a small beginning to the life-long process of working cooperatively with the Holy Spirit.

The doctrine of regeneration allowed Spener, and subsequently other Pietists, to cling to faith alone as the basis of and motivation for action in the ethical life. The motivation to be good or to love well in the framework of faith initially comes from God alone. Yet the ongoing, or regenerative, nature of our faith requires us to be co-participants with Christ through the work of the Spirit. From this three-fold structure, the Pietists affirmed Paul's motto in Galatians 5: All that matters is faith acting in love. God works through faith; we participate in love. We now turn to the ways that we grow our faith in order to act in love.

The Serious Business of Baptism: Indoctrination

Indoctrination is a bad word among Christians who want to be loving and tolerant of other Christians and other faiths. It doesn't have to be, however. Really, when you think about it, why would we Christians *not* want to know what we believe and believe what we know? Why would we resist rigorous formation in the faith? None of us can expect to be good at being Christians without continually challenging ourselves and the content of our beliefs. Spener's ministerial practices of catechesis, conventicles, sacraments, and preaching help us to think of indoctrination as training in Christian character or as being formed and challenged in the faith that we receive. Indoctrination is a good word. It includes those habits of faith that Christians cultivate over time to be more excellent at trusting God.

Catechesis

When Spener was appointed to the most prominent preaching position of Chief Court Preacher in Dresden, the joke was that the Elector called a court preacher and got a schoolmaster.[6] Spener was a teacher, and at the heart of his pastoral ministry was instruction in the faith, or catechism. Catechism teaches the basics of faith and doctrine. Beyond this, it places us in the trajectory of God's work in the history of the Christian church. Spener thought that Christians needed instruction throughout their lives. He challenged adults, and published *The Spiritual Priesthood*—a "study guide" for reading Scripture. In it, he systematically worked through the responsibilities and identity of the common priesthood with the aim that the whole church could better exercise its priestly functions. Whether children and youth, adult and elderly, the Christian life gets its vitality when we continue to be formed in the faith, and Spener's reforms in this area were substantial.

Most of his contemporaries taught so that learners would come away with knowledge of doctrine. Not Spener. He taught matters of doctrine, certainly, but he had two other, more pressing, concerns. First, he wanted people, especially children, to come away better able to read their Bibles. He

6. Spener, *Spiritual Priesthood*, vi.

was committed to confirmation and to teaching young people the beliefs of the historical church so that they might have a lens to apply what they read in Scripture. His second goal was relational—Spener saw catechism as a way for his parishioners to hear the living voice of a pastor who communicated God's truths in Scripture. This relationship was not merely an approach to catechism, it was also, Spener believed, the content of the gospel.

Spener's passion for catechism came as a result of those theologians and clergy who trained Spener. The Lutheran efforts to catechize were, strangely, absent. Spener thought catechism was a critical activity that cultivated strong faith, and he thought that the hearts of youth were great fields to be sown and plowed.[7] Furthermore, he connected catechesis directly to baptism. Catechism was the church living out its commitment to raise and form youth in the faith. Though youth were the focus, he also thought that adults should actively keep up their own learning. Without ongoing Christian formation, adults—even those who grew up in the church— would not grasp the fullness of the gospel in life-giving ways.

The importance of catechism as a habit that promoted the excellence of faith became ever more clear in Spener's understanding of worship and liturgy.[8] In worship, we rehearse the story before God. Worship allows us to give God our best rendition of the story and to practice the plotline we ought to live throughout the week. Spener understood that the ability to recite the creeds and know correct doctrinal formulations were simply not enough to live the story well. He firmly

7. Stein, *Philipp Jakob Spener*, 80.

8. For a more in depth study of Spener's liturgical reforms, see Johnson, "Pietist Theology of Worship."

believed that the story had to reside within the hearts and minds of the faithful. He knew that outer faith without inner life would *not* do what the evangelistic mission of the church was supposed to do, namely live a life that witnesses to the truth of Christ. He thought that one way to incorporate the inner and outer aspects of faith, or the knowledge and practice of faith, was through worship, and so he attended to key ritual aspects of the worship life of his congregations as an extension of catechism.

The historical context offers further insight into why the connection between catechesis and worship was so important for Spener. In his day, worship was, by aesthetic standards, done well. However, aspects of worship remained in the charge of only a few people—clergy and professionals such as musicians. Worship was not participatory, stunting what Spener thought was a key component of good evangelical worship, namely holistic participation of both head and heart. While the congregation knew and enacted all the mechanics of worship, Spener saw little soul and conjectured that this was in large part due to the fact that lay people did not understand what was happening. They did not, for example, think about how the third article of the creed (recited in worship) might have bearing on daily life. Or, why it was so important for lay people to read Scripture in worship. Spener begrudged the disconnect between knowledge as rote recitation and knowledge as formation, and sought for a convergence by using catechism to fortify liturgy and worship. Catechesis, he believed, made Christians better able to integrate theology and practice, which in turn gave persons the ability to move from faithful worship to faith in daily life.

Conventicles

Imagine that you are a pastor who decides to take a risk and preach two provocative sermons. The first sermon is an admonishment, in which you call the majority of your congregation Pharisees because they live in the belief that they will be saved simply because they are part of the evangelical faith. The second sermon is a charge, in which you suggest the good effects that might be born in a parish whose people come together in their free time to study the Word and to edify one another. You might expect to get some calls on Monday morning with harsh sentiments toward your first sermon. Or, in the case of your second sermon, you might find that your parishioners complain that you are asking far too much. Spener's congregation did neither. Instead, a small group came to him and asked for opportunities to delve together into Scripture in order to strengthen their faith. The purpose, they told Spener, was to learn the truths in Scripture, to more fruitfully apply Scripture to daily life, and to come together in a spirit of love. Most pastors would see this as a cherished opportunity, the result of difficult yet faithful preaching, and that is exactly how Spener responded when the parishioners of the Lutheran Church of Frankfurt-am-Main approached him.[9]

Through experiences such as these, Spener became a champion of conventicles, or small groups that gathered together apart from the Sunday worship to discuss the texts for the day and the sermon. He argued theologically for conven-

---

9. For more on Spener's sermons and the scholarly conversation surrounding their role in the creation of conventicles, or *collegia pietatis*, see Stein, *Philipp Jakob Spener*, 85–87.

ticles, and they were central to his first proposal in the *Pia Desideria*.

> Thought should be given to a *more extensive use of the Word of God among us*. We know that by nature we have no good in us. If there is to be any good in us, it must be brought about by God. To this end the Word of God is the powerful means, since faith must be enkindled through the gospel, and the law provides the rules for good works and many wonderful impulses to attain them. The more at home the Word of God is among us, the more we shall bring about faith and its fruits.[10]

Conventicle gatherings began with two primary goals. The first was simply to read Scripture together and reflect on its meaning for life. They pondered questions of faith, hope, and love and sought to apply those to Christian living. They truly believed that the Word was a double-edged sword, living and active, and powerful enough to penetrate the heart of the believer. Reading Scripture together gave more opportunity for the Word to penetrate their lives and for the Holy Spirit to transform them more deeply in the faith.

Secondly, conventicle gatherings served as a place to edify one another and the community as a whole. Spener created a safe environment for his parishioners to converse and allowed only conversation in which they spoke positively about one another. Spener sought not to engage in idle talk, gossip, or any form of grievance that was negative in tone. He believed that the power of the spoken Word generated faith,

---

10. Spener, *Pia Desideria*, 87.

and that the power of the Holy Spirit working through mutual edification generated hope and love.

In "A Treatise on the Affections," an appendix to his guide to the reading and study of Scripture, August Hermann Francke also paid heed to the role of the affections in reading Scripture and made a number of pertinent points. One was that when we read Scripture faithfully, we submit our hearts and minds to be amended and corrected. Admonishing one another need not be done by speaking critically to one another but by speaking in a way that uplifts and encourages another to desire to *be* good or to respond more faithfully next time. Francke also pointed out that love is the first fruit of the Spirit and source of Christian transformation. Together, love and submitting oneself to be transformed in community are the heart of mutual edification. We can more easily confront difficult truths when we are secure in our love for one another. It is good to know that my brother or sister in Christ desires what is best for and most fitting to me. We are edified by one another in order to be lovingly transformed, and this transformation is brought about both by the practice of loving and being loved. It is the environment within which faith can grow. Spener made a concerted effort to provide such a forum for reflection on the content of faith as well as an intentional community for habituating edifying behavior.

The result was that conventicle gatherings quickly grew and expanded the boundaries of the priesthood. Spener took in all interested persons, and eventually this included persons who were uneducated and members of the lower classes. The mixing of social classes became a powerful indentifying mark both within and without the conventicles. Within, Christians found a unifying identity, namely their baptism in Christ.

Conventicles were one of the only places where the social classes came together without regard for class distinction and saw one another as equals in status. They believed this was how God saw them. In this way, baptismal identity was not merely preached, it was also practiced by encouraging individual Christians as well as the ecclesial body to take on a whole new identity as a family of faith. From without, conventicles were seen as an open, inclusive group of people. For this reason, they evoked much suspicion among both civil authorities and Lutheran clergy. The conventicle effort to mix classes was perceived as a threat to social standing and political order and an attempt to disempower the ordained clergy. Spener saw neither complaint as valid. He strove to cultivate a strictly Christian identity and unity among his parishioners. As to charges among the Lutheran clergy, he understood his conventicle efforts to be aimed at growing a strong priesthood whose end was to serve as ministers to the world.

The fate of the conventicle movement in Germany was mixed. Some continued to flourish after Spener took a post in Dresden in 1686. Some, however, broke off from the Lutheran church—an outcome that Spener deeply lamented. Criticisms from without grew, and while Spener continued to hold to the core structure and identity of the conventicles he began, the fact that some groups strayed too far from the church caused Spener some distress over how best to support lay conventicle gatherings. Sadly, he discontinued his conventicle efforts when he left Frankfurt. Nevertheless, his devoted efforts in concert with his parishioners remained a model for cultivating the virtue of faith in Christian community, and in the end, Spener advocated for conventicle gatherings as a strong exercise of the common priesthood.

Sacraments

Spener's theology of the sacraments might be summed up by the unitive function that the sacraments play. The sacraments unite Christians by making them one with Christ and with all who share in God's promises and blessings. Baptism is the ritual of grace that achieves unity by bringing persons under the fold of the church's care. Spener believed baptism was also regenerative, in that it gave persons the beginning of new life. A life of unbelief negated or distorted the promises held within baptism to the extent that new birth was lost (although never beyond retrieval) and Christian unity was compromised. Spener's approach to baptism was to see it as the visible sign of God's grace that served Christians both outwardly (as an act of grace) and inwardly (as a predisposition to or welcoming of the work of the Holy Spirit). He thought baptism should call those baptized to the highest response of faith and hence the deepest forms of Christian living. In baptism, we are born anew, and, as Jesus tells Nicodemus in John 3, we are born of water and the spirit. We are justified, sanctified, and given the power to live as new creatures. Spener affirmed this view of baptism and called his parishioners to a regenerate faith in the form of continuing to receive—or say "Yes!" to—faith. This "Yes" to God found roots both in the believer's baptismal identity as a child of God and in the community's vows and commitments to one another. As we saw in the examples of status in conventicles, baptismal identity played out in the life of the church in practical ways.

Spener understood communion as the place where the seeds of faith and the soil of formation were fed. Christ is the food that gives Christians life, and Christians are nourished when they accept the body and blood of Christ in faith. The table was representative of this movement in the Christian life and served to invigorate Christians through the bodily, outer reminder—the bread and the wine—of the spiritual, inner grace. In communion, Spener held that Christians were strengthened in faith to love their neighbors. Communion was both an outward physical act and an inward spiritual one. Receiving communion was also a witness of a faith that apprehended God's Word in body and spirit.[11]

Spener's insistence on joining the inner and outer in the sacraments underscores the mechanics of virtue, through which the excellence of character corresponds with the good act. Sacraments—especially communion—are habitual ways that we see and are reminded of these holy mechanics. At the table of the Lord, we regularly practice communing, and in the Eucharistic habits of asking forgiveness, sharing food, and receiving grace, we nourish the excellence of faith. Beyond this, the sacraments are places where we celebrate, and in doing so habituate ourselves to the vision that they represent—Christ's body unified.

In presiding over the sacramental life of the church, both Spener and Francke were aware that the font and the table were places that the common priesthood gathered without regard for class or station in life. To this end, they administered the sacraments in two distinct ways that embodied this unity and that exemplified the ethical dimensions of faith. Contrary to the common practice of having a separate cup for the wealthy classes, Spener and Francke insisted that all persons—regardless of class—partake from the same

---

11. Spener in Stein, *Philipp Jakob Spener*, 221.

cup when receiving the sacrament of communion. Likewise, they insisted on a common font, as opposed to the acceptable baptismal practices of alternative water for the wealthy. These liturgical changes recalled Gal 3:28, that in Christ, social categories are erased when Christians come together as one around the table and around the font. Spener's sacramental administrations allowed his parishioners to habituate themselves to the unifying benefits of faith.

Preaching

Perhaps the best scriptural example of Spener's theology of preaching as he sought to cultivate faith as an excellence and a practice is Jesus's Sermon on the Mount. The prologue to Jesus's sermon goes something like this. After having called his disciples, Jesus travelled through Galilee. In synagogue and street alike, Jesus preached the good news of God's kingdom. Great crowds came to hear him and in hearing him, they were healed of their woes—diseases, unclean spirits, troubles, and pain. Those crowds were aware of Jesus's power that *healed all of them* according to the scriptural account.

In the gospels, preaching is connected to ethics. Hearing is linked to doing. The prologue on preaching gives way to the beatitudes—the encounter with the blessings that describe the excellences of Christian character in surprising ways. Those who are poor, hungry, meek, merciful, and pure in heart receive the kingdom of heaven, and in turn, they exemplify the character of the kingdom promised. Excellences such as meekness, for example, predispose persons to act in ways that embody God's kingdom on earth by resisting retaliation in the face of another's wrong-doing. Jesus's sermon paints a picture of many other such actions that emerge from the character traits above. Interestingly, hearers and doers cap the sermon. Jesus ends his sermon by addressing the hearers and doers—those who hear his words and do not do them will fall. Unheard, the foundation of faith is rendered useless, because unheard translates into undone. On the other hand, blessed are they who hear the good news and respond in faith, for it is in *hearing* the gospel that we are given excellences from above and enact the kingdom of God.

The connection between hearing and doing greatly influenced Spener's theology of preaching. These two—proclaiming the good news and hearing the good news—linked the preacher and the congregation together in the ongoing formation of faith. Proclaiming the good news was never easy, in Spener's mind, and the best sermons were those that were clear, accessible, and understandable—traits many preachers and teachers alike find difficult to pull off. As Spener's sixth proposal suggested, preaching is for the edification of the congregation, and if the congregation cannot understand the sermon, they will not hear the good news.

Spener's second concern for preaching was doing, or application. He hoped that the congregation would be transformed by the hearing of the Word—that those who heard would then have the capacity, or excellence of character, to apply the good news to their lives. Hearing renders persons capable, for God works in and through the proclamation, thought Spener. Good preaching awakens people's faith! Good preaching sows seeds of knowledge which in turn bear fruit! Good preaching edifies the congregation, so that they are built up! Good preaching opens the heart, allowing Christ to work in it! Spener believed this about preaching, and he wanted his parishioners to hold him accountable, largely in conventicle conversations, to good preaching that was edifying for the whole priesthood.

Spener's theology of preaching assumed a strong pastoral relationship with all parishioners and especially the poor and less educated. Spener believed that the poor needed to have access to proclamation of the Word because they were best suited to receive the gift of faith and best suited to live a life dependent on God. The peasants were in the best position to hear and understand the gospel in large part because examples of love in Scripture came from the lowest classes. In addition, throughout Scripture, partiality was given to the poor. *Blessed are you who are poor, for yours is the kingdom of God.* This emphasis conditioned the content and rhetoric of Spener's sermons.

Moreover, his attention to the lower classes shaped the way that he believed sermons should function in everyday life. Spener was able to paint a picture of how the poor should be treated and empowered, and he proceeded to "do" that which he heard in the text. He promoted the establishment of the "Poor, Orphan, and Work House" in Frankfurt, and he sought to find work for those who had none.[12] Wherever he ministered, Spener demonstrated his knowledge of and advocacy for the "least of these"—widows, orphans, peasants, unemployed, refugees, migrants, beggars, and invalids. He encouraged his parishes to work as Christians in partnership with the government to provide things like aid, jobs, relief, homes, and medical care. James Stein describes well the social results of Spener's pastoral efforts in Berlin.

12. Ibid., 239.

In 1695 the elector created a relief fund for the
poor and forbade begging. That same year a spin-
ning mill began to employ the able-bodied poor. In
1702 the great Friedrichs-hospital was completed.
Two years later it was meeting the needs of 1,996
individuals. For a few years the beggars disap-
peared from the streets.[13]

Spener utilized the pulpit in connection with the common
priesthood to motivate the church on behalf of the poor and
to include the uneducated classes of Germany in the whole
ministry of the church.

CONCLUSION

In the *Pia Desideria*, Spener wrote about renewed faith. "The
Word of God remains the seed from which all that is good
in us must grow. If we succeed in getting the people to seek
eagerly and diligently in the book of life for their joy, their
spiritual life will be wonderfully strengthened and they will
become altogether different people."[14] The Christian ethical
life is about becoming an altogether different people, and
faith is a primary gift God gives his people toward this end.
The people's job is to respond in belief as Spener sought to do
throughout his life. How should we believe? As the gospels
of Matthew and Mark conclude, Believe and be baptized! Go
and make disciples by baptizing people and teaching people!
Spener chimes in this gospel chorus: Believe by putting our
baptism into constant use throughout your lives!

13. Ibid., 240.
14. *Pia Desideria*, 91.

The end of the moral life is, for the Pietists, evangelistic. How should we believe? We believe by cultivating faith so that we may live lives that paint a portrait of the gospel. Upon closer examination of Spener's ministry, the more directly ethical answer might be: Believe by extending the common priesthood of believers! Spener's ministerial emphases—catechism, conventicles, sacraments, and preaching—challenge us not only to *know* the God in whom we believe but to use our faith for the mission of inviting and including those who have not yet heard or those who do not fully participate in the church's ministry. For Spener, an expanded priesthood was largely about inviting those of lower classes to participate in the full ministry of the church. The extended priesthood was the practical outcome of the excellence of faith cultivated over time through habit. An extended priesthood is the living example of the idea that faith is both an excellence and a response: We have faith (*pistis*) and we believe (*pisteuō*).

In his theological biography of Philipp Jakob Spener, James Stein asserts that Spener's greatness lies not in his creation of a new denomination, nor his liturgical change, his theological writings or his contributions to hymnody. His greatness, rather, lies in his self-chosen role as a "renewer of a sluggish state church; a proponent of a vital faith relationship with Jesus Christ that far exceeded the customary expectations of respectable church life and one that could effect meaningful changes in the stuff of everyday existence."[15] Spener lived in the faith extended to him when he was baptized into the family of God. He also died in faith. On February 15, 1705, the parish of St. Nicholas Church celebrated Spener's death

15. Stein, *Philipp Jakob Spener*, 5.

and new life in the kingdom of glory. A service proceeded without eulogy and laud, because Spener wanted the congregation to worship God not memorialize his own life. And so, the good news was preached, and the resurrection was given color—for Spener was buried in white, symbolizing his baptism into eternal life and faithfully proclaiming, in death, his hope for a renewed Church on earth.

QUESTIONS TO CONSIDER

1. What is your own story of faith? How do baptism and conversion function, and how do they relate for you?

2. What is your experience of Christian education and formation? How does your church meet the needs of children, youth, and adults? How do or might Christian learning experiences integrate various age groups?

3. What is the role of preaching in your formation?

4. What are the various ways your church reads Scripture together? Reflect on those and consider ways you might be challenged.

5. Have you considered faith as a virtue that Christians continually habituate themselves to? How do you understand the connection between faith and ethics? How might you continue to strengthen that connection?

THREE

How Should We Live?

"It is a sign of our love that we keep your commandments."
—Johanna Eleonora Petersen

Johanna Eleonora Petersen converted to the faith slowly. She was born into a Christian home, yet she travelled in circles that practiced Christianity as a culture more than a life of discipleship. She had neither the kind of educational opportunities that Francke enjoyed, nor the kind of formational guidance that Spener received, and so Petersen came to faith slowly because conversion—including repentance and a radical turning toward God—was not the norm. She needed something other than her cultural climate to stimulate her faith. She needed a glimpse of the kind of love that breathes new life into dead faith. She needed to experience the Word made flesh. She needed to witness faith acting in the kind of love that bears all things, believes all things, hopes all things, and endures all things. These are what it took for Petersen to call herself a converted Christian.

This chapter addresses the question, "How should we live?" The short answer is, we love. If faith is the virtue that points to the gospel, love is the virtue that embodies the gospel. Of the three theological virtues—faith, hope, and love—

love holds open the door to conversion, to new life, and to lasting communion with Christ. It is the Word made flesh. Charles Wesley said it well in the first stanza of "Love Divine, All Loves Excelling":

> Love divine, all loves excelling,
> Joy of heavn' to earth come down;
> fix in us thy humble dwelling;
> all thy faithful mercies crown!
> Jesus thou art all compassion,
> pure, unbounded love thou art;
> visit us with thy salvation;
> enter every trembling heart.

This hymn appeals to both Christians and non-Christians to make their hearts a humble dwelling for Christ, the "joy of heaven to earth come down." It is about the divine love that upon conversion begins to transform the excellence of love in us, making us capable of loving others. As the hymn also suggests, God's love is a love that never ends.

Love opens the door to the gospel, and we cultivate the virtue of love by keeping God's commandments. Jesus knew that love embodied the gospel when he said, "'You shall love the Lord your God with all your heart, and with all your soul, and with all your mind.' This is the greatest and first commandment. And a second is like it: 'You shall love your neighbor as yourself'" (Matt 22:37–40). These two commandments are the hinge from which all else hangs. Love God, and love your neighbor. One of Jesus's clearest teachings, this directive gives life and breath to our faith. Love is the connective tissue between human beings and God and between human beings themselves. Whether characterized as deep reconciliation between sinners, gentle compassion for those grieving, or reverent worship of God, love is a gift, and when we cultivate it by obeying Jesus's command, we hold open the door for others to see the truth of the gospel. If we believe, as chapter 2 suggests, by taking our baptism and Christian formation seriously, we love by taking our conversion, or new life in Christ, seriously. We obey this greatest command to love God and love our neighbors as ourselves.

Johanna Eleonora Petersen was an exemplar of Jesus's double command to love God and neighbor, and her devotion to God opened doors for many would-be and seasoned Christians. Her devotion also, interestingly, opened the door for her own conversion. Petersen's life is known mostly through her own spiritual autobiography, or love letter to God. It describes her ongoing conversion as the anchor of the Christian life. It also reveals how she came to love God and others by reading Scripture. As well as any other early Pietist, Petersen's story moves us into the heart of the double love command as it embodies the gospel.

The Knock on the Door: Conversion and New Life

In the medieval home of the widow Maria Julian Baur, new life was born. Women started reading their bibles. In seventeenth-century Germany, the religious culture of the day adhered to what they still interpreted as Paul's injunction against women speaking in church. Outside of the church, small group Bible studies, or conventicles, consisted only of men, and women who did show up were not allowed to speak or be seen. Seeing that faith might be enlivened by the activity of reading Scripture, Johanna Eleonora Petersen (née Merleau) challenged the conventicle movement to allow the participation of women. With Spener's encouragement, Petersen began the Saalhof Pietists—the first conventicle gathering where Frankfurt women engaged their Bibles actively. They read, prayed, and learned, in essence, to speak their faith. As this devotional gathering came to life, the Word took on flesh in Frau Baur's home, and women's participation in the faith experienced a kind of birth.

Petersen led the way for women to articulate their faith for themselves. In a sense, she was a midwife whose passion for reading Scripture allowed her to help others give birth to their faith in a way that was personal and powerful. How did she get to this point? Why was Petersen so impassioned by the Word? What does her passion for Scripture have to do with the excellence of love?

Petersen grew up in a poor family of nobility, meaning that she had status but not wealth. Her childhood was marred by the death of her mother, whom Johanna loved, and by the civil struggles associated with reconstructing Germany after the Thirty Years' War. Her father was a strict man, disappointed that he was left with four girls and no heir. He hired a number of women to care for his daughters. These women did so haphazardly, even negligently, and when Johanna was twelve, she was sent to live with Countess Barbara Maria von Solms-Rödelheim. The Countess was sick and suffered from bouts of depression making her incapable of caring for Johanna. Johanna's father then moved her to the home of her godmother, Duchess Anna Margaretha, to be a lady-in-waiting. In the home of the Duke and Duchess, Johanna traveled in interesting social circles, learned the ways of the world, and enjoyed what was for her a generally happy time compared to her former years. While she experienced a sense of place and rootedness for the first time, Johanna struggled inwardly. She had reason to be cynical about life. She suffered losses, moved around, and lacked a sense of purpose and identity. She had reason to run from, instead of to, God. However she did not. Instead she struggled to be faithful and exuded a kind of patience with her circumstances that allowed her to remain steadfast in her pursuit of faith.

After living with the Duchess Anna Margaretha for a number of years, Petersen became accustomed to the pleasures in life—good food, beautiful clothes, and decadent parties. Yet, faith continued to tug at her heart. Clergy and laypeople found her a pious lady in the midst of her extravagant lifestyle, but she did not see herself as a true follower of Christ. In her autobiography, Petersen wrote,

> There was no one who said [my life] was not right, but everyone praised such vanities and considered me blessed and pious, because I read, prayed, and went to church and was often able to recapitulate the sermons in every detail. [. . .] This pleased everybody. I was considered a pious lady by all, clerics and laypeople, although I led a life with love and desire for the goods of this world. I had not yet entered the following of Christ.[1]

Petersen realized that her loves were distorted, and that she did not love God above all else. She realized that the seeds that were planted in her by her mother's faith had not yet seen

---

1. Petersen, *Life of Lady Johanna*, 70.

any fruits, so she began reading Scripture to explore the tugging on her heart.

A few years into her time with the Duchess, Petersen met Philipp Jakob Spener during her travels. They talked for hours, and she knew she was in the company of a serious Christian. Their conversation, as she described, became an impetus for Petersen to commit her life to following Christ.

> We entered into a spiritual conversation that lasted several hours. . . .We talked together without stopping and it was as if [Spener] were looking into my heart and everything that had given me doubts until then came out. Not a word was lost that was not in God's spirit. I remembered all when the time came for actual practice. Yes, I found in this friend what I had doubted would exist in anyone in this world, because I had looked for so long to see whether there were true active Christians.[2]

Petersen saw in Spener not only wisdom, but humility, meekness, mercy, and holy love. She left their time together comforted and divinely persuaded. She had entered new life in Christ, and what was once primarily a devotion of outward actions became a devotion of her heart.

For Petersen, hearing the faith journey of another opened the door for her own love for God. Spener's story affected her inwardly, penetrating her heart, mind, and soul. She later described her conversion neither as a deep crisis that moved her to God nor as the result of the kind of ongoing faith formation that had nurtured Spener. She described her conversion as a function of God tugging on her heart through

2. Ibid., 74.

the Word and of the Holy Spirit enlivened in the testimony of a man who deeply loved God. After her conversion, she asked to resign from her duties, arguing that she could not in good conscience continue living her current lifestyle. Petersen knew that her position with the Duchess afforded her neither good examples of Christ followers nor an environment that would cultivate Christian excellences. Her path was not easy. The Duke and the Duchess, together with their patrons and ministers, challenged Petersen. All wanted her to stay. None could fathom her inner conflict. Petersen, however, was resolute. "I was," she wrote, "commanded to *choose the best*."[3] She believed that a mediocre attentiveness to Christian faith and piety were not, in fact, the best that God wanted for her life.

After a brief interlude in her father's home, Petersen received permission to take up residence with the widow, Maria Julian Baur. In her home, Petersen seriously took up the discipline of reading Scripture. Petersen did many things to increase her knowledge of Scripture. To begin, she learned the biblical languages. She found a Frankfurter Jew who could teach her to read Hebrew. She subsequently learned Greek. She also became active in conventicle gatherings, which eventually led her to initiate the Saalhof Pietist group that included women and men. Finally, she wrote many theological works that integrated her faith with the narrative of Scripture. Petersen's passion for reading and reflecting on Scripture was rooted in her experience of loving God. She cultivated a personal relationship with Christ, and her work brought together her love for God and her love for her neighbor around the activity of reading God's Word.

3. Ibid., 77. Italics mine.

At this point it is worthwhile to examine some of the ways that Petersen incorporated her love for God and her love for her neighbor through three of her scriptural disciplines. First is her spiritual autobiography that chronicled her conversion to Christ. Petersen's narrative placed her loves under the microscope of Scripture with the intent to witness to the power of God's love. Pietist scholar Dale Brown calls individual conversion stories such as Petersen's the "seed" for the language of revivalistic Pietism. Second are Petersen's theological writings, or what I call her epistles. These were her writings about God in the form of conversations with other believers. They sought to edify the community of faith and to illumine the light of Christ in the believer. Her method was visionary, and the way she spoke about God revealed her personal experience of Christ and the application of Scripture to life. Third is Petersen's teaching and conventicle activity. Her response to new life in Christ was to read the Bible in small groups, allowing the Holy Spirit to transform her. Each of these disciplines was inspired by the double command to love God and neighbor, strengthening the connective tissue of the people of God and expanding the common priesthood. Far from being an individualistic theology of experience, Petersen's work shows us how the personal dimensions of faith do, in fact, edify the whole church.

JOHANNA ELEONORA's "CONFESSIONS"

Evangelicals have always been inspired by stories of conversion. Whether they be in the form of the *Confessions* of St. Augustine, a sermon such as Billy Graham's, or the testimony of a new or mature Christian, Evangelical Christians unite around the plot of conversion. Conversion stories proclaim the good news of how individual believers have come to love God, and such accounts have a powerful way of binding Christians together.

In seventeenth- and eighteenth-century Germany, spiritual autobiographies were the primary mode of telling conversion stories. Spiritual autobiographies testified to the ongoing spiritual regeneration in the life of the believer. Written in the genre of St. Augustine's *Confessions*, Pietist autobiographies were avenues for individual Christians to tell their stories and for uniting them around the common theme of loving God. Petersen's own spiritual autobiography was such an account. Hers was the first known autobiography to be published by a woman in German. As we saw in the preceding section, her narrative included the events leading to her conversion and was structured around her ongoing spiritual development.

Spiritual autobiographies brought about unity in the priesthood in two ways. First, readers gained windows into the journey of other believers. Spiritual autobiographies were not private diaries that persons kept to themselves. On the contrary, they were circulated within an extensive communication network. The Pietists had rich exchanges between themselves and various groups all over Continental Europe and into England. They corresponded frequently through letter writing, and cross-communication between various groups, including Quakers, Moravians, German Lutheran and Radical Pietists, was common. Through these communications, readers learned about the struggles and joys of Christians and about ways that God was working in the lives of those who loved him.

In many sections in her autobiography, Petersen emphasized her reliance on God and her struggle to love others. From the perspective of one who had personally experienced the depths of sin, she wrote about diligently praying that God would forgive and have mercy on her brothers and sisters. Petersen had many friends, and she also had enemies—usually described as those who slandered her and persecuted her for her faith. Nevertheless, she prayed for them. She used her affection for God to transform her disdain for her enemies. She wrote about her transformation—about times when she tasted love for her enemies, so much so that she wanted to take that love into her heart and carry it with God. "My love," she wrote, "was very deep when I realized that I gained more from [my enemies] than from my best friends."[4] Petersen never romanticized or glorified her love for her enemies. Instead, she wrote of the difficulty each and every time someone committed an injustice toward her.

> But no hour is like the next, and often it may happen that at first we do not feel with such a love what happens to us unjustly, especially if we have not experienced it for some time and have been quiet. Then we have to *learn anew* how to love our enemies and to accept everything from the hand of the Lord. This has happened to me so often that I have to turn back again and explore thoroughly the benefit of this or that suffering before I can accept it and bear it with joy.[5]

Petersen's description of love for her enemies is an example of how love for God can spill over into love for others—even those who have ill will toward us.

Those who read her spiritual autobiographies were affected by them. Readers saw models of Christian living and

4. Ibid., 84.
5. Ibid.

paradigms for understanding conversion and regeneration.[6] Those who read them were edified. Detailed personal descriptions of God working, on the one hand, and stories of moments when God was absent, on the other, served to edify those who struggled with their own faith. In writing personal conversion narratives, Pietist spiritual autobiographers shaped the movement and the character of renewal in the church by drowning the body with examples of God at work.

In addition to offering windows into the journeys of other Christians, spiritual autobiographies unified the priesthood by creating a sense of membership and ecclesial belonging. This was in part due to the fact that their stories contributed to the ethos of the movement. It was also, however, due to what German scholar Peter Vogt calls envisioning the "Cloud of Witnesses." In his article on Pietist discourse and the invisible church, Vogt claims that communicating experiences of conversion through the circulation of spiritual autobiographies created a communal identity among readers and writers. Because they were so widely read, it greatly enlarged the sense of Christian community beyond local gatherings. The cumulative effect, writes Vogt, was an experience of the Communion of Saints or Cloud of Witnesses. Moreover, he points out that the experience of being in communion with other Saints transcended not only geography but history as well, because they were also reading historical works such as those of St. Augustine, Thomas à Kempis, and Teresa of Avila.[7]

6. For an excellent article on the communal functions of spiritual autobiography in early modern Germany, see Vogt, "In Search of the Invisible Church," 293–312.

7. Ibid., 305.

When we reflect on a spiritual work such as the *Confessions* of St. Augustine, we see the power of a well-written testimony in creating intimacy with other Christians. Because of Augustine's candid telling of his journey to Christ, readers feel as though they know him somewhat intimately. This kind of intimacy was also operative in Pietist autobiographies, and their honest reflections on their devotion to God created a sense of belonging to one another through their common love. In the example of Petersen's spiritual autobiography, her love for God not only gave her readers a sense of intimacy with her, but she also came to have greater intimacy with others along the way.

JOHANNA ELEONORA'S "EPISTLE"

The oeuvre of Johanna Eleonora Petersen is remarkable in both its breadth and its style. Because she was a layperson (and a woman), she had to write in a more devotional and visionary way. She could not take up issues of doctrine as her male contemporaries, including her husband, could. Many of her contributions came by working collaboratively with her husband, Johann Wilhelm Petersen, under whose name she could speak more doctrinally. This did not stop her from writing and publishing in her own name, however, and over a period of thirty years, she published in excess of fourteen religious books.[8]

Her visionary writing style integrated her spiritual journey with theological insights based on her reading of Scripture. While her autobiography centered on her conversion experience as testimony, her theological writing utilized

---

8. Petersen, *Life of Lady Johanna*, 28.

her experiences to speak more directly about God. I call them epistles because many of them were. Her style was dialogical, and her writing took up difficult questions about God, such as: What does discipleship in response to Christ's passion look like? Why is it that Christians, who are people of peace, wage wars among themselves? What is the relationship between the two natures of Christ? How is Christ present in the Lord's Supper? Whom does God, who is essentially love, save? What are God's plans for the Jews?

Petersen wrote from her experience but never without the aid of Scripture. While her work took up doctrinal questions, it was not considered to be formal theology. Her tone often had a more ethical flavor. Her devotion to God, her relationships with others, and her reading of Scripture informed her experience and hence her lens for talking about God. For example, in a work that addressed God's relationship to contemporary Jews, Petersen's claims lifted up the importance of the role of the Jews in salvation history. She exhibited a clear disdain for any form of anti-Semitism. God, she wrote, has great plans for the Jews, and it is the commission of all—Jews and Christians alike—to turn toward the God of Scripture and to experience a "holy change" because of it.[9] She advocated both the chosen place of the Jewish people along with the exhortation that Christians were to live the mission of Christ by loving the Jewish people. This example, and many others, showed Petersen's attention to doctrinal questions as they were integrated, or lived out, in the life of the believer and the church as a whole.

9. For more on this, see Jung, "Johanna Eleonora Petersen," 155.

At this point let us examine one of Petersen's works, a letter that she wrote to her sisters on the subject of being a new creature in Christ. The heart of the letter, called "The Nature and Necessity of the New Creature in Christ Stated and Described according to the Heart's Experience and True Practice,"[10] was that those who love Christ are transformed by Christ. They are new creations who pursue love. The content of Petersen's letter—reconciliation and brotherly/sisterly love—and the mode in which she wrote—an epistle to her sisters—testified to the integrative manner in which she loved God and others. Love for God, she indicated, does not come naturally. Love must be practiced. It must overcome sin through practices of repentance and unity. The underside of life, she wrote, comes out in a daily way through regular confession. Sin exists even in the lives of those converted, and by asking for forgiveness, we open the way for renewal of self and unity with others. This, wrote Petersen, constitutes much of the practice of love.

Her occupation with sin and repentance was not unusual among Pietists. They have, in fact, been criticized for their harsh views on sin and evil. I would suggest, however, that the Pietists demonstrated courage in the face of a culture that downplayed the role of sin in the life of believers. Whether a result of an overly optimistic view of human nature or of a singular focus on the once-and-for-all nature of the atoning work of Christ or of the aftermath of a church obsessed with indulgences, sin was a less important doctrine in the seventeenth-century German church. Petersen and other Pietists were not afraid to confront the power of sin and to

10. Petersen, "Nature and Necessity," 103.

use Scripture for these purposes. By placing sin in the context of daily repentance, directed doubly to God and neighbor, Petersen both acknowledged the presence of sin and situated it in the realm of God's forgiveness. Sin was addressed within the narrative of the gospel—a gospel that both confronts and forgives.

The ability to look sin directly in the eye and practice loving our neighbors through forgiveness is the soil of a unified faith. When they spoke of unity, the Pietists were referring to love. Like Spener, Petersen desired unity in the church. Unfortunately, dispute over doctrine often divided the body, and Petersen was outspokenly critical of this. Doctrine, she believed, was meant to be lived and to bring us more deeply into love of God. The church should be a place of enduring love—where those who believe in the message of the gospel come together to worship God and to be co-participants in Christ, regardless of theological differences. Theological differences ought to be a source for growth, an impetus for transformation, or a reason for renewal. When the body is divided—whether by sin or by theological differences—Christ's community is broken, and love breaks down. Petersen wrote that the connective tissue in the midst of division needed to be love, for when people commit sin or express diverse views, love is the excellence that makes us capable of enduring one another. Love, she thought, is cultivated over time when we bear one another's sins, believe in God's good news, sustain hope in the power of the Holy Spirit, and endure the messiness that is humanity. Sometimes, love sits in the filth of life, but, as Petersen's letter concluded, sin and division are never the end of the story for those who love Christ.

Petersen's letter ended with a benediction to her sisters. "So run then, dearest sisters! that ye may obtain. And be you hereby, from the very bottom of my heart, commended to the Love Eternal."[11] She concluded by reminding her sisters that all God's commandments are lovely, and that none of God's commandments hinders human happiness. Being commended to the Love eternal is what humans were created to become. God intends the best for his children, and Jesus's double command to love God and neighbor is precisely that best.

JOHANNA ELEONORA'S VOCATION

One of the most faithful ways Petersen loved her neighbors was by reading, teaching, and preaching the Word. Self-educated, Petersen read widely and explored theological questions with those who, like her, wanted to think through the Christian faith. While living with Frau Baur, she educated young girls in reading Scripture. Frau Baur ran a boarding school from her home, and Petersen taught a small group of girls every day. In addition to other general subjects, Petersen taught the children to memorize Scripture and read devotional works. With the older ones, she even ventured into Greek.[12] Girls were not otherwise exposed to Scripture in such a direct manner, and Petersen equipped them for a life of reading and learning.

As I indicated earlier in the chapter, Petersen also began the Saalhof Pietist group—a group that broke off from the larger *Collegia Pietatis* gatherings in Spener's home in order to form a group where women could read and reflect

11. Ibid., 119.
12. Ibid., 7.

on Scripture. Petersen gathered regularly with the Saalhof Pietists, and they discussed their faith together. Because women were part of the group and because they explored a wide range of theological questions, the group experienced much resistance by civil authorities and Lutheran clergy. Petersen defended the group successfully enough to maintain the gatherings over a period of five years, to the delight of those who regularly gathered.

Petersen also took up preaching later in her life. She preached at religious gatherings and, some speculate, in Pietist church services.[13] Throughout her life, she had memorized sermons, particularly Spener's, and recited them verbatim. She quickly learned the skills of preaching well, and she applied them when the movement was more strongly underway. The state forbade her to preach, of course. Nevertheless, she continued to do so even though preaching brought dissention from those outside of Pietist circles.

Petersen's mature and active faith fed her ability to love well. In Ephesians 3, Paul prays, "I pray that, according to the riches of his glory, he may grant that you may be strengthened in your inner being with power through his Spirit, and that Christ may dwell in your hearts through faith, as you are being rooted and grounded in love" (Eph 3:16–17). Petersen's habits of reading, teaching, and preaching Scripture strengthened the excellence of love within the priesthood in two related ways—first, by inviting greater participation of lay people, and second, by including women. The Lutheran Church had a unifying structure in its doctrine and in its worship life. However, laypeople were increasingly relegated to roles

13. Ibid., 17.

that did not require them to engage their faith. Theology, for example, was done by the theologians. Leading worship was left to the clergy. Interpretation of Scripture was dependent upon the preacher. While these roles were in many ways appropriate to the office of ordination, the practice of faith was so limited to the clergy that not only did this bifurcate the common priesthood, it also became nearly impossible for the church to experience what Luther and Spener referred to as an enlivened faith. Petersen's example was significant because she understood her vocational boundaries within the realm of God's gifting. With the support of many Pietist friends, Petersen faithfully stewarded her gifts for the good of others, and in doing so, she suggested new possibilities for lay people to engage in the ministry of the church. Moreover, Petersen modeled new roles for women, and those previously on the margins of church and society became actively involved in their spiritual development. In the perspective of German scholar Barbara Becker Cantarino,

> Petersen gave voice to Pietist women; she [. . .] helped prepare the way for women's individual and collective expressions in the religious community and beyond. [. . .] Petersen articulated her spiritual experience, while most remained silent, and created a body of devotional and religious texts as an exegesis of *the* book, the Bible.[14]

The practice of reading and reflecting publicly on Scripture had heretofore not been open to women, and this new opportunity strengthened the way women understood and lived the Christian faith. As active participants in their spiritual

14. Ibid., 43.

growth, the outcome was that they became, as Paul writes, rooted and grounded in love.

As a whole, the Pietist movement was supportive of this new door for women in large part because they were people unified by a book—the Bible. What was so critical about this new door, however, was not simply that women pushed the boundaries of ecclesial and social restrictions, although expanding gender roles in the Pietist movement was indeed an important hallmark. Even more exciting was that women's engagement with Scripture challenged their faith and worked in their lives in new ways.

CONCLUSION

Love is the door that opens the way to the gospel. Augustine's love letter to God concludes with an open door. "From you let it be asked. In you, let it be sought. At your door let us knock for it. Thus, thus is it received, thus is it found, thus is it opened to us."[15] Petersen's own spiritual autobiography also concludes with a door. "When I began to raise my voice . . . the door opened and I felt very well . . . God has become visible." In Scripture, the knocking goes both ways. In Matthew's gospel, we are told to knock. "Ask, and it will be given you; search, and you will find; knock, and the door will be opened for you. For everyone who asks receives, and everyone who searches finds, and for everyone who knocks, the door will be opened" (Matt 7:7–8). In Revelation, Jesus does the knocking. "Be earnest, therefore, and repent. Listen! I am standing at the door, knocking; if you hear my voice and open the door, I will come in to you and eat with you, and you with me"

15. Augustine *Confessions* 13.38.53 (Ryan, 370).

(Rev 3:19–20). In each of these instances, the door opens the way to good relationships with God and others. The double command to love is woven throughout Scripture—it is the hinge from which all else hangs—and if you were to continue to read the Scripture texts above, you would find that both passages concern themselves with how we love God and how we love others.

How do we live? We love. We answer the knock on the door that invites us to enter into communion with God and with others. Luther wrote, "Faith brings you to Christ and makes Him your own with all that He has; Love gives you to your neighbor with all that you have."[16] Love, according to Luther, has its source in God's invitation to us. The life of Johanna Eleonora Petersen frames this invitation well. Her love for God was the source of the way she gave herself over to her neighbors. Her enduring efforts to know God through Scripture cultivated her love. In the previous chapter, we addressed the virtue of faith in such language as knowing God as the content of our faith, living into our baptismal identities, and strong Christian formation with the aim of believing in, or trusting, God. Faith, however, must be known by its fruits. Faith is not simply the input of truth and knowledge. As the Pietists proclaimed, faith acts in love. How did Petersen exemplify "faith acting in love"? In a word, she joined love of God with love of neighbor. As her spiritual autobiography showed, she never lived as though her faith was private. As her theological writings showed, she found God by loving her neighbors and praying for her enemies. As her disciplines of teaching, reading, and preaching showed, she lived a life of on-

16. Luther in Forell, *Faith Active in Love*, 101.

going conversion to God, and in doing so she was receptive to others. Her work was so effective that she played a significant role in extending the priesthood to include women, changing how they saw their roles in the church. Petersen organically brought together the double imperative to love by answering the knock of Christ and by showing the door to others.

The double love command draws us out of ourselves and into communion with God and neighbor. Reading Scripture is critical in cultivating this love because it gives us the narrative context to understand what it means to give ourselves over to our neighbors. Conversion stories are life-giving because they provide us windows into the faith journey of others. Writing and reflecting, or some form of spiritual discipline centered on God's word, are essential because they turn us toward God. These are habits that cultivate the excellence of love. The results are that we can bear one another in our theological differences, we can endure each other with enough strength to forgive even our enemies, and we hope long enough to be reconciled to God and one another. How do we live? We love, and in bearing, believing, hoping, and enduring, we open the door to God's saving work. In this way, love never ends.

Questions for Reflection

1. If you were to write your spiritual autobiography, what events would you highlight? How does love guide you in moments of struggle? Of joy?

2. How has the conversion story of another brother or sister in Christ inspired you to live more faithfully or called you more deeply into a life of discipleship?

3. What biblical texts have been especially formative for you? Why?

4. What are ways your congregation tells stories? What are some of the stories or experiences that define your congregation?

5. Have you thought of love as a virtue? What practices do you engage in that cultivate the excellence of love? What does it mean to give yourself to your neighbor in love?

FOUR

How Should We Hope?

"And thus he then goes forth into the struggle in faith and does not become tired, but waits with patience and hope, full of faith for the day of his setting free and the appearance of the great God and our Savior Jesus Christ and the crown of eternal life which he will surely receive from his hand by grace."
—August Hermann Francke

August Hermann Francke converted in a grace-filled instant. In one moment, he had fallen on his knees to God in prayer, begging for hope and salvation. In the next, he arose with overwhelming joy and great assurance, praising the God who had shown him great grace. Francke's story of conversion, which I tell in more detail below, is a story that is full of doubt and assurance, tears and joy, struggle and hope. Francke was not a man to do things halfway. When he was in the world, he was erudite. When he was in the church, he was pious. When he cried, he sobbed. When he was joyous, he praised God. When he converted, he gave himself over to God and neighbors, and upon his conversion, he began an earnest pursuit of the Christian life.

This chapter asks, "How should we hope?" The short answer is, we hope by pursuing heaven on earth. As did other

Pietists, Francke pursued hope vigorously. The charge that opens this chapter, however, does not necessarily indicate vigorous pursuit or a man who understands hope: "Wait with patience and hope for the crown of eternal life!" Christians who care deeply about suffering in the here and now might be tempted to turn a deaf ear to these words. The charge indicates great glory for those who wait patiently, not those who act definitively. It describes a future day when Jesus will appear, and the faithful will be crowned, not heaven on earth. It hints at a "not yet" posture toward the world to come—a future crown of eternal life. On the flip side, the above charge does not speak to issues of poverty. Nor does it not make promises about ending world hunger. There is no mention of a strategy for dealing with issues such as creation care. On the face of it, it does not even offer much motivation to act on behalf of the least of these.

Nevertheless these words are not without hope in this life, not without attention to justice in this world. Anyone who has read about August Hermann Francke knows that he lived and breathed the kind of hope that pursued heaven on earth. While Spener reformed the church, Francke sank efforts into social reform as an extension of the church in the world. Francke exerted patience not by doing nothing, but by patiently enduring. When he hoped, he did so faithfully, and, as we will see in the subsequent pages, while he waited for the eternal crown, he rebuilt earthly cities with a vision of the heavenly.

Hope is a difficult virtue to articulate clearly, and thus prone to misuse or misinterpretation. Often, evangelical discussions of hope turn into doctrinal formulations or other-wordly speculations disconnected from our lives in the here and now. There are Christians who spend more energy calculating the exact day and time of the rapture or looking for signs of Revelation 20 on people's wrists than they spend calculating how much of their income they could live without or how they might significantly decrease their daily refuse. After all, some say, why bother? In the end, it all passes away, right? Such views on the end times, or the present time, can lead to overly spiritual or overly despairing frameworks for doing the work of Christian ethics. Given their emphasis on spirituality and, at times, their chiliastic approach to the end times, Pietism has suffered from these charges of hyper-spiritualization.

While Pietism emphasized spirituality and mysticism and Spener took a chiliastic approach to the end times, Pietist hope is a lost treasure in the church's history. The hope of the Pietists inspired a resuscitation of personal faith and widespread renewal in the church. The Pietists practiced hope as the virtue that enabled them to look backward and forward, up and down. Hope needs history for guidance, and it needs the future for vitality. Hope is the temporal virtue that frames—backward and forward, up and down—the life of the church in the here and now. It looks up to the angels and down to the worms. It combines the glory of God and the good of our neighbor. It brings together faith and love. How should we hope? We hope by attending to earthly life in a manner worthy of the gospel. We hope by rebuilding the earthly with an eye toward the New Jerusalem.

Spener was known for this kind of hope—so much so that he was buried in white, as we saw. The subtitle to his *Pia Desideria* was "hope for better times." Petersen also lived in hope, particularly in the hope that by reading Scripture, God's truths would continue to become clearer. She hoped that love for God would transform the world and bring people to Christ. Francke was no different. In Francke's life and each of its phases, one uncovers an embodied hope that integrated heaven and earth and that assumed the connection between this life and the next. Francke has many stories, and in this chapter, we consider virtue of hope through three phases of Francke's life—the story of a man, the story of a church, and the story of a school.

THE STORY OF A MAN . . .

As I indicated earlier, Francke knew the moment when he was converted, and it was not as a child. He grew up in Gotha, a center of Pietist thought, and his parents were pious people. His father introduced him to the writings of the Pietist grandfather, Johann Arndt, including *True Christianity*. He read devotional literature and knew Luther's catechism. As Francke remembered, his parents had theological aspirations for him. In spite of these many early Christian influences, Francke described himself as having idle ways in his youth, as following the bad examples of other children, and as being ignorant about the real state of his faith.[1] His sister remained a strong, Christian grounding force for him, but Francke was easily blown by ways of the powerful in society, and he knew that his worldly ways impeded his capacity to live out his faith in any genuine way. In the words of Petersen, he knew he was not yet following Christ.

Learning was at the forefront of Francke's early life, and the academic environment wooed him from the start.

---

1. Stoeffler, *Evangelical Pietism*, 185.

His father was a lawyer, and later in his life he assisted in the reconstruction of Saxe-Gotha under Duke Ernst. His mother was the daughter of a mayor and came from a family of wealth. Their social status enabled Francke to receive an excellent education, including private tutors and schools. At the University of Erfurt, Francke continued his studies, finding much joy in the world of books and academics. He wrote of his interest in scholarship and advancement, of his vanity with respect to the world, and of being comfortable with what he described as the easy living that accompanied progress in one's studies.

Prior to his conversion, Francke wrote in his autobiography,

> In such circumstances my life pleased the world to such a degree that we were able to get along very well together, for I loved the world and the world loved me. I was therefore very free from persecution because among the pious I had the appearance of being pious, and among the evil I was truly evil; I had learned to let my cloak blow in the direction the wind was blowing. [. . .] Nevertheless such a peace with the world was not able to bring any rest to my heart.[2]

The state of Francke's faith continued to nag at his soul. He studied Bible and theology and attended church—including confession and communion—regularly. He was able to distinguish between worldly ways and desires and Christian virtues and piety. Yet, he believed that he lacked a "heart" experience of theology and faith. He questioned his motives, knowing

2. Francke, "From the Autobiography," 100.

that they were neither for the glory of God nor in service to his neighbors but rather for his "own glory and profit."[3] Because he did not love God and questioned his affect toward others, Francke continued to examine himself, but to little avail.

When Francke was twenty-four, a friend called Francke with an invitation to live in Christian community. Francke accepted, and soon after his arrival, his friend asked Francke to preach on John 20:30–31: "Jesus performed many signs . . . written so that you may come to believe that Jesus is the Messiah, the Son of God, and that through believing you might have life in his name." In the time between preparation and preaching, Francke confessed to his friend that he had no faith. That evening, Francke knelt in prayer to God, crying out for salvation from his miserable state. After years of prayer and self-examination, Francke's heart was moved. God finally heard Francke, and changed Francke's heart. Francke felt such a stream of joy that he immediately stood up, praising and giving honor to God. He later wrote, "I arose a completely different person from the one who had knelt down."[4] He continued, writing that as he had knelt down, he had not believed there was a God. When he arose, however, he had neither doubt nor fear that God was one in whom his heart could rest. In the light of the resurrection, Francke arose a converted man, and at the age of twenty-four, Francke was born again.

Francke's conversion became the fire of his heart. His story is one example of how persons come to living faith and how faith immediately works to transform persons. Francke's conversion united Francke's intellectual gifts with his passion

3. Francke in Sattler, *God's Glory*, 24.
4. Francke, "From the Autobiography," 105.

for action and his heart for change. In addition, his conversion was perhaps the impetus for his pastoral call, the story to which we know turn.

. . . THE STORY OF A CHURCH . . .

In 1692, in the city of Glaucha, Germany, hope seemed impossible. Glaucha lay in eastern Germany up until the early twentieth century. It neighbored the slightly more reputable Halle and harbored what Jesus might have called "the least of these"—those who could not escape from political and social ills. Poverty, prostitution, and homelessness defined Glaucha's state of affairs. In postcards, children's books, and history books alike, depictions of Glaucha in the late 1600s contained similar themes—those of poorly nourished children, intoxicated men, and scantily-clad women. Glaucha was not, by any standards, considered a city of hope. The streets were filthy, the homes were in shambles, and the education system was almost non-existent.

In the middle of all of this, however, the small parish of St. George's opened its doors every Sunday. And people came. They were not always sober or clean or prepared for worship, but they showed up. They often arrived late, left early, let their children run free—but they showed up. They just needed a pastor, and Philipp Jakob Spener, then-president of the consistory of Berlin, appointed August Hermann Francke to the post.

When Francke took the call to go to St. George's, he was also professor of Greek and Oriental (Hebrew) Languages at the new University of Halle. Because his income was tenuous, he accepted the call to St. George's. Unbeknownst to Francke, an interesting development occurred as a result of accepting the dual posts of professor and pastor. Prior to Francke's appointment, the offices of pastor and professor had existed as distinct professions.[5] With his appointments, Francke brought the two together in a way that combined the training of pastors with the practice of ministry. In other words, teaching Bible and theology became more than simply an academic endeavor that required university training. Teaching was also about the experience of ministry and the ability to apply classical disciplines to the daily life of the church. This was a significant development within Pietism, and both Spener and Francke were committed to integrating academic rigor, the experience of faith, and the life of the local congregation to the end of a strong spiritual priesthood. For St. George's, this meant they got both a well-educated pastor and a man whose heart lay in the interests of his people. Francke ministered at St. George's with enthusiasm and found that the vocation he once feared—that of being a pastor—in fact added life to his love for theology and Scripture.

Francke's ministry at St. George's lasted over a decade. Throughout his tenure, he made numerous efforts to care well for his people. He began strong programs of catechism, he preached often, and he made frequent pastoral visits. He reoriented his congregation to consider holidays as extra days for worship. He practiced great hospitality by hosting conventicles and by passing out food to the poor at his door. Within two years of his pastorate, he opened the doors of his home, and, in addition to handing out food, he proceeded

5. For more on the history of the relationship between these offices, see Martin Schmidt, *Der Zeitalter des Pietismus*, as cited in Sattler, *God's Glory*, 46.

to teach them Luther's catechism. Why not, he had thought, share the gospel with them in addition to feeding them? It is what Jesus himself called us to do—feed people both in body and in spirit. So, the ritual of food and instruction for the poor became a weekly event in Francke's home, and it showed Francke's deep commitment to the life of the church and the neighborhood.

Francke's attention to the poor and to the social issues contributing to poverty came to the fore in his ministry at St. George's. When he arrived for the first time, his heart broke when he saw the conditions in which people were living. He described Glaucha as the pits.

> Halle did not make a particularly good impression [. . .] streets and squares were either poorly paved or not paved at all. All the houses were of the same uniform yellow color. All the garbage was thrown in the streets. A street ordinance of the Elector expressly forbade dumping dead cats and dogs, blood from slaughtered animals, and manure from the stables in the streets. Twenty years later an order of the King required the paving of the entire city. Glaucha, with its two thousand inhabitants, was even dirtier.[6]

His pastorate, more than anything, prepared him to address the conditions and undertake the kinds of radical reforms that would benefit the people of Halle-Glaucha.

In 1697, the first Sunday after Trinity Sunday, he delivered one of his most hopeful sermons, titled "The Duty to the Poor." In it, he preached that Christians might better prevent the groans of the poor and the wretched by imagining car-

6. Francke in Sattler, *God's Glory*, 38.

ing for them in ways that glorify God. He framed all material goods by saying that God gives them to us so that we might use them to help our poor, suffering neighbor. Earthly resources are first obliged to the poor. This duty, Francke went on to preach, concerns each and every Christian. It excludes no one. And our experience of sharing and inclusion at the Lord's Table trains us for this duty. The net Francke cast around his definition of who constituted the poor was great. It included those who had nothing by way of material goods but it also included those who could not help themselves, those who were home bound, and those who were in pain or distress. Most significantly, as the gospel said, the widows, the orphans, and the sick belong under the care of the Christian church. Finally, Francke exhorted all Christians to a daily accounting. He asked all to tithe, and he asked all to give things up, to practice abstaining, to listen to the poor, and to account for how we spend all money and use all goods. Everything Christians do, Francke preached, is to be motivated by sincere love for the poor.

Christians today might be greatly edified and challenged by Francke's sermon. It was both simple gospel truth and a challenging call to steward our gifts lovingly. Above all, it was a hopeful sermon that addressed the most devastating social ill in human history, namely poverty. Francke truly believed that, by the grace of God, Christians could affect the plight of society's "least." His sermon ended with the prayer:

> Ah, Lord! Give us that we truly change and from now on receive a new heart and new mind, and because it is your mind, that you are love itself as you have described yourself to us when it says "God is love," ah, so help us by your grace, you who are love

itself, that we may all experience in our hearts your divine mind, to love our neighbor as ourself [sic] as you have given us a commandment through our Lord Jesus Christ, who loved us unto death! Amen! Amen!

Francke preached and lived in hope, and the church of St. George's became God's instrument of justice in the streets of Glaucha.

Today St. George's church still stands in what used to be the "red light" district of Glaucha. It is now part of Halle and a few blocks from the Francke Foundations. One Sunday evening, in the spring of 2009, our family attended worship at St. George's. With the exception of the computer equipment in the back of the sanctuary and the overhead screens, it looked as one might have expected it to look three hundred years ago. The sanctuary was filled with a variety of people from seemingly diverse socioeconomic backgrounds. Children were running in and out of the service. A woman was helping a man suffering from a hacking cough to his seat. Though they had already begun worship, we were immediately greeted by not less than three people. On the whole, there was a combination of worship and hospitality enacted in various ways in the course of the evening. We learned that about sixty years ago, the church was on the brink of closing. However, an Evangelical Free church plant had found a home in the church of St. George's. They slowly grew, and they are now working on building renovations. In 1692, St. George's was a place where hope seemed impossible. In 2009, we found, in fact, that God's instrument of justice—the church—continues to live in hope. And while the exterior of the church was filthy, the Christian formation rooms in a state of disrepair, and the sanctuary in need of work, the people at St. George's continue to build.

. . . AND, THE STORY OF A SCHOOL

"Poverty," Francke wrote, "is a stain upon our Christianity. The bond of holy brotherhood is torn apart through the deficient piety of Christians."[7] After Francke became established as a professor and pastor, he tackled deep-seated social problems. He introduced many reforms in his lifetime, but most significant were his educational ones.

It began on Thursdays. Every Thursday night, Francke invited the poor in his neighborhood to a food and catechism gathering in his home. In a short time, Francke realized that one night a week of hospitality and Christian formation were not enough for those who had little by way of food and education every other day of the week. He decided to leave an alms can in St. George's in order to generate funds to do something about the lack of education among the poor children. Francke, like Glaucha in 1692, needed hope. There was simply too much to do with too little resources, and this alms can was a first attempt to address Francke's lack of resources. When the alms can did not fill up, Francke—somewhat frustrated and doubting the ability to effect significant change—went to God in prayer. Turning to Corinthians, Francke heard, "And God is able to provide you with every blessing in abundance, so that by always having enough of everything, you may share abundantly in every good work" (2 Cor 9:8). God spoke to Francke in this verse and gave him some fruits of hope. Francke received God's Word and let the passage in

7. Francke in Sattler, *God's Glory*, 49.

Scripture work on him—enough so that Francke began to think in terms of the abundance promised in 2 Corinthians. He began to develop a more thorough plan for reform. Soon after, Francke found an offering in the alms can—an amount estimated to be around seventy dollars.[8] Francke joyfully took the money. He used it to buy books for children, and in 1695, he formally began a poor school—the *Armen-Schule*—in his home.

The progression of Francke's poor-school reveals Pietist hope as it allowed the heavenly to interface with the earthly. Francke relied on heavenly abundance by hearing God's Word and by using his gifts and training for the good of others, particularly children. Francke also relied on the abundance of God through the generosity of others. Without these abundances, Francke would not have been able to build a school. With these abundances, the concerted efforts of God's people expanded the priesthood to include one of the neglected social groups—children. Soon after he began teaching poor children, the school quickly grew, and more and more children were educated and formed in the Christian faith. Within months, the parents of middle class families realized the quality of Francke's educational program and asked if they could send their own children.[9] Eventually, word spread to the families of nobility, and by the end of the first year, Francke was educating the children of both the poor and the wealthy, allowing the tuition of the wealthier families to carry the expenses for the poorer ones. Everyone, it seemed, won. Children from all classes received an excellent education, Francke's school gave Halle increased influ-

8. Gary Sattler estimates this amount in Sattler, *God's Glory*, 50.

9. Ibid., 51.

ence in the surrounding areas of Germany, people continued to give Francke money, and, most importantly, the priesthood continued to grow.

Francke was known for having a risky faith. He never carried a reserve fund. He quickly spent all of the money he received on the poor. He refused to accept confessional money that the penitent typically offered to their pastors. As we might imagine, his finances suffered over the years, and the orphanages lived from donation to donation. Nevertheless, they kept the doors open.

Francke definitely took risks—but he did so in hope. Francke oriented himself to live in the kind of hope that believed God would bring creation to completion. He believed deeply in the first article of the creed—that God is the maker of all that is, seen and unseen. Even when Francke struggled, which he did especially as his influence grew, he acted as though hope would manifest itself somehow and in some way before the end of the day. This is how God spoke to Francke in 2 Corinthians 9, and so he continued to live in the hope that God would give abundantly. Francke believed nothingness was no obstacle for God, and he was able to connect with other priestly people who also believed nothingness was no obstacle for God. We see a moving example in a letter Francke received from a widow who offered her small yearly proceeds to the orphanage. Understanding her gift as a response to the first article of the creed, she wrote to Francke, "The one who can make something out of nothing proves it also in the small and lets it be blessed. Amen!"[10]

10. Weborg, *Eschatological Ethics*, 85.

And so, in a spirit of hope, the school continued to grow and flourish. Francke's desire that children would learn to love God and live for God's glory and the neighbor's good framed all that he did. His approach to learning was holistic, in that he thought that children should not merely be taught but also formed to have good characters. In the end, he wanted to evangelize the head, heart, and spirit of those whom he taught.

Education was the primary mode through which he lived and breathed his faith, but he also engaged in other reforms. He established widows' houses, advocated for prison reform, and included girls in his education programs. His influence extended into Prussia, and Francke developed a friendship with King Frederick William I. Their collaborative relationship benefited Halle Pietism because Frederick William gave them unprecedented opportunities for social reform. Their relationship also benefited the Prussian state because Francke's social work and Pietist theology influenced Prussia's social restructuring in the early eighteenth century.[11] Finally, Francke's Halle activity inspired many missionary movements, and Pietism became a vehicle of the gospel in the Baltic states, Russia, and India.

While Francke and the Halle Pietists engaged in good work both abroad and locally, perhaps the pinnacle of Francke's work was the opening of the *Stiftungen*—or Foundations that included a larger orphanage and schools. The staff included supervisors, a pastor, administrators, and teachers. From what we can gather in the wonderful descriptions of Gary Sattler in

11. For a well done study on the relationship between Halle Pietism and the Prussian state, see Gawthrop, *Pietism and the Making of Eighteenth-Century Prussia*.

God's Glory, Neighbor's Good, [12] building the new orphanage
was a crowning witness of God's abundance. The orphanage,
which still stands in Halle, resembles a kingdom more than
a home for poor children. Originally, it was constructed out
of stones and bricks donated by the court of Brandenberg-
Prussia and shared by a castle in Berlin. Orphanges had, in the
past, been described as "snake pits," distinguishable neither
from shoddy workhouses nor from penal institutions. [13] This
orphanage, however, paralleled some of the best architecture
of its day—a highly unusual mark for a building whose purposes were to serve the least of these.

The orphanage-school marked its dawning neither by
the day its founders broke ground nor by the day its builders
set the roof, but rather by the day its mission was inaugurat-
ed—on the day the children *ate*. On Easter morn in the year
1700 orphans and students shared a meal out of which grew
the mission of forming and educating children.

The architecture of Francke's buildings are physical signs
of Pietist hope, and they play an important role in the story.
The beautiful baroque façade on the face of the building well
matches the dignity of the school's mission and the residents
who have passed through it. When one approaches the face
of the *Stiftungen*, one is met by a grand staircase that beckons
one to enter and to explore that which is behind its doors.
The hall where the children ate, attended lectures, and heard
concerts was built with many windows where the light continually makes its presence known. The library is filled with
Romanesque arches, under each of which are rows of books
accessible for those in pursuit of knowledge. The architecture

12. Sattler, *God's Glory*, 62.

13. Ibid., 61.

signifies hope and has contributed to the formation of the character of the children who have lived within their walls.

Those who hope build. And build, Francke did. He built orphanages, welcomed the widows and beggars, and effected social change. He reformed schools for children of all classes, included poor girls in his educational innovations, and responded to other social needs, turning Halle into a thriving city of social reform. Often, he did so without funds, without support, without even a good plan—hence Francke's designation as a man of "risky faith," or, to be more precise, a man of "hopeful faith."

CONCLUSION

The Francke Foundations is alive and well today and is a great example of hope reaching backward and forward. The Foundations continue to offer schools for children of all ages. The Foundations have also begun an intergenerational home. The Orphans' Garden continues to grow, and the library still stands as it was built in the 1720s. On the wall of the Great Conference Hall are pictures of the seventeen directors of the Francke Foundations between the years of 1700–1946. Latin is still taught, and the Cabinet of Curiosities—where Francke collected various artifacts from around the world for pedagogical use—is now a museum.

However, much has also changed. Part of the grounds suffered damage from World War II bombings. During the Soviet occupation of East Germany, many of the buildings became dilapidated and were impinged on by the fly-over constructions and high rises. Following the reunification of Germany in 1990, the Board of the Friends of the Francke

Foundations re-established support from the state of Saxony-Anhalt and began restoration.[14] During this time, much was revived, and the place is a flourishing witness to enduring hope. In conjunction with the Martin Luther University, it houses the most extensive Pietism Archives in the world and the Interdisciplinary Center for Pietism Research. A former dairy is now a workshop for training unemployed persons in the trades of carpentry and painting. In sum, what was once the place that sent the first Protestant mission, the origin of Christian social welfare work in Germany, and the site of educational reform for children of all ages now includes day nurseries, a children's creative center, music schools, a "House of Generations," a Bible center, a training center for the unemployed, a university, and research institutions. What was in the early 1700s literally known as a "New Jerusalem" is today still a "New Jerusalem."

As Francke's life exemplifies and the ongoing nature of the Foundations testify, hope is not waiting patiently—hope is what enables us to wait patiently. Hope, as an excellence, is that strength of character that lives patiently in the midst of human sin and brokenness. As such, hope cannot subsist without faith, or the knowledge of our God and Creator. As an action, hope is the enactment of the content of our faith. Hope is participating in building the earthly kingdom with an eye toward the heavenly. The heavenly kingdom, in other words, is the blueprint from which we build. God is the architect, we are the "builders."

How should we hope? We hope by having faith that God will bring creation to fruition and by allowing love to work

14. Raabe, *Guided Walk*, 9.

in such a way that we give ourselves over to our neighbors. The first part of how we should hope entails a patient waiting with the knowledge that we live in the mystery of faith, between the claims "Christ has risen!" and "Christ will come again!" The second part of how we should hope encompasses the vastness of love—it encompasses love with a vision. The previous chapter ended with the statement that love is an end in itself. Hope addresses the fact that while love is an end in itself, it is never complete until Christ comes again. Because of human sin, hope acts in such a way as to give content and context to *faith acting in love.* If faith points to the gospel and love opens the door to the gospel, hope brings them together. Hope glorifies God by rebuilding earthly cities with an eye toward the New Jerusalem.

QUESTIONS FOR REFLECTION

1. Reflect on Francke's prayer following his sermon "The Duty to the Poor" or another prayer that you find hopeful. How often do you experience hope through preaching and prayer? How does prayer move you to apply the exhortations of a sermon?

2. What are ways that you do an "accounting" of your gifts of time, money, and resources. How might you improve your stewardship? How are you intentionally accountable to the Christian community?

3. What spiritual disciplines do you practice that orient you to people who Jesus calls "the least of these"?

FIVE

Conclusion: Faith, Hope, and Love

"Quite simply remember you would 1. believe, 2. do, 3. hope
what is taught, commanded, and promised in Scripture."
—August Hermann Francke

This Companion has been largely a celebration of the early German Lutheran Pietists and a reflection on their ethic in light of their remarkable theology and practices. The intent was to tell their stories in order to show that the ethical life is inherently a matter of Christian habits and Christian character. I began the book by comparing Pietists to Hobbits, and I confess that one hope I had was that readers would become endeared to the Pietists, not unlike those who read Tolkien and become endeared to Hobbits. In telling their stories, I sought to connect my Evangelical brothers and sisters with our historical Pietist roots as they call us to a life deeply formed by the Word. Pietists cherished aspects of the Christian life that Evangelicals also cherish—the importance of personal conversion, an attention to social issues, an excitement for missions both locally and abroad, and, most importantly, the centrality of the Bible for Christian community and the practice of faith. The Pietists' work as a renewal movement in the church has much to offer Evangelicals today. They challenge us to ask: Do we live lives that point to the gospel of Jesus Christ and expand the boundaries of the common priesthood of believers?

RE-VISITING THE BOGEYS

This book ends by reminding readers that the biographical witnesses to the questions of How should we believe?, How should we live?, and How should we hope?, are events of receiving God's great gifts of faith, love, and hope and cultivating them through simple Christian habits. By way of reminder, I revisit some of the "bogeys" of Pietism in order to show how the Pietists' renewal efforts offer a corrective for a variety of struggles that the Evangelical church faces today. In the following sections, I address three of what I call the "bogeys of Pietism" as they correspond with the primary questions and theological virtues that organize this book. These are: (1) the bogey of faith as too subjective and individualistic, (2) the bogey of love as too emotional, and (3) the bogey of hope as too otherworldly.

The Bogey of Faith as Too Subjective and Individualistic

The first bogey is the claim that Pietism is too subjective, focusing almost solely on the individual while neglecting the established church and, in some cases, civil authorities. Indeed, the subjective dimensions of Pietism are part of their story, and they primarily appear in such practices as reading the Bible, the experience of personal conversion, and conventicle gatherings outside the Sunday worship service. The subjective character was also fostered by empowering the laity to be greater participants in their own faith, as seen, for example, in how Petersen accepted functions previously reserved for ordained ministers. It must be remembered, of course, that each of these practices was a corrective to a church that seemed on the brink of falling asleep. The new emphasis on a personal relationship with God was an attempt to bring life to a dead church. Conventicles were an attempt to gather more frequently around the Word, to read more of the Bible than the lectionary offered, and to hold ministers more accountable to preaching. Never did Spener desire for practices that enlivened individuals' faith to cause a separation of groups from the whole church, and he lamented when divisions occurred.

What has been forgotten within the allegation that Pietism is too subjective and individualistic is that it kept the faith of individuals within the context of the faith of the whole church. Pietists preserved the communal context by emphasizing baptism as the marker identifying the individual as a child of God and part of God's family, the church. They kept subjectivity in check by attending to the content of the church's faith—by catechizing and forming believers in the historical practices of the church. They continued the Protestant heritage of preaching the gospel faithfully and administering the sacraments regularly. Moreover, they read Scripture often and understood God's Word to be the center of the Christian faith. What has been forgotten is that the emphasis on subjectivity and on the individual occurred in the context of a community that understood itself to be part of the whole church and a participant in the ongoing work of God through the church in history. When that context is forgotten and when we remember only the corrective, we overlook the balance between the individual and community.

The Pietists' practice of faith has a lesson for Evangelicals: we need to know who we are and to whom we belong. Identity is everything. The simple answer to who we are is, we are Christians—children of God and a priestly people, called by Christ for the work of the church. Unfortunately, it is easy to forget or water down our Christian identity when there are so many other identity markers in our culture. Pietists remind us to ask how the primary marker of "Christian" makes a difference for us as men, as children, as business ex-ecutives, as plumbers, as 9s on the enneagram, as leaders, as Americans, as Republicans, as people. The Pietists remind us that "Christian" is an essential marker of our identity, and as such, all of the other descriptors not only take a back seat to our unity in Christ, all other descriptors—whether cultural, biological, or vocational—must be understood in light of our common faith. If we are family, as our baptismal vows claim we are, then we can joyfully identify with Christians every-where based on the fact that we have the gift of faith in Jesus Christ.

The Bogey of Love as Too Emotional

The second bogey is the claim that Pietism is too emotional and that Pietists' affective reading of scripture made their the-ology biased and even sectarian. The emotional dimensions of the Christian faith are part of the Pietist story. In cases of Radical Pietist groups, the emotional emphasis took over in the form of aesthetic mysticism, visions, and prophetic tendencies. It should be noted that some groups also leaned toward anti-intellectualism and separated from established religion and churches.

Among the early Pietists, such as those this book has focused on, the emotional emphasis is most evident in their view that conversion entails an affective turning toward God in repentance. While conversion is in part a rational assent to the gospel, conversion also requires that persons are open to being convicted by the Holy Spirit of their own sin. Persons need to be, in a sense, emotionally receptive to God transforming them. Furthermore, the Pietists placed great emphasis on the role of the emotions in the interpretation of Scripture. The Pietists believed that well-formed affections aid Christians' ability to read Scripture. Francke's "Treatise on the Affections" argued that readers ought to understand the affect of the writers of Scripture because that would give Christians more insight into the world of the text and the message in it. In addition, if readers of Scripture want to glean the kernels of truth, they need to be converted Christians, and they need to welcome the aid of (and sometimes surprises of) the Holy Spirit. Only those truly oriented to God can see the truths God has revealed in his Word. The emphasis on the emotions was a reaction against a highly rationalized and intellectual faith and an attempt to encourage Christians to engage God holistically.

What has been forgotten in the allegation that Pietism is too emotional is that the aim of an emotional approach to God was conversion and a life of ongoing regeneration. The Pietists did not mean for the Christian life to be a sustained emotional high, as such charges often indicate. On the other hand, regeneration indicates a holistic transformation with emotional dimensions. This means *both* the rational and affective qualities of being human are engaged and transformed by the ongoing work of God in the life of the believer. The Pietists' attention to the emotions did not negate the development of the mind, and we saw very clearly that Spener, Petersen, and Francke were all devoted students of the Bible and theology. Nor did the attention to emotions serve as a sectarian device. The Pietists strongly advocated for the emotions connecting the ecclesial body because emotions emerge, originally, from a deep love for God.

The way the Pietists practiced the virtue of love has a lesson for Evangelicals: loving God is a matter of the heart, the soul, and the mind, and it deeply shapes *how* we become a priestly people. Loving God is an affective, Spirit-filled, and intellectual engagement with God's revelation in Scripture. What does this mean? It means we engage God through our emotions. Sometimes we are in love with God. Other times we are angry with God. Still others, we are afraid of God. Each of these affective dispositions is present in the Bible, and all are honest human responses that ought to be used as multidimensional lenses for approaching God. Loving God with heart, soul, and mind also means that we are open to the work of the Holy Spirit. This openness comes by way of submitting ourselves to the community of faith and confessing our sins to one another—not just the little ones but the ones from which we need real freedom. Openness comes by way of listening to how others read Scripture perhaps differently than we do, hearing stories of how our brothers and sisters experience conversion in daily ways, and reflecting on God's promises and commands in light of our own lives. Loving God with heart, soul, and mind means, finally, that we engage our faith with intellectual discipline. We read theology, we learn what history has taught us, and we engage worship with our heads not just our hearts. Loving God is the essence of conversion. Far from a one-time emotional event or decision, conversion is the ongoing lesson that moves us to love our neighbors as ourselves.

The Bogey of Hope as Too Otherworldly

The third bogey is the claim that Pietism is too otherworldly and that Pietists live in the heavenly realm while denying the earthly. While some Pietists, including Spener for a period, had strong premillennialist worldviews, in general these functioned more to ensure an urgency for evangelism and missions, rather than to encourage a neglect of the material world. It is true that Francke had some preoccupations with lists and rules that seemed to call persons to a kind of impossible otherworldliness. For example, in his "Scriptural Rules of Life," he told Christians not to burden their hearts with cares about food, not to waste time caring for the body or looking in the mirror, and not to plan life around happiness. It is also true that Spener lived an aesthetic lifestyle and was constantly aware of avoiding excesses, under which he would have included dancing and drinking. We can also note that Petersen converted to Christ because she saw the worldly behaviors of her peers and decided that those behaviors were not God's desires for us. Of course, we must remember the context. For all his rules (which, by the way, he followed himself), Francke stood out from other, far more strict, headmasters. Unlike they, Francke allowed children to play and to laugh. For all his temperance, Spener did enjoy beer on a regular basis. And for all Petersen's criticisms of worldly behaviors, we must remember that most Christians in seventeenth-century Germany considered themselves Christian because citizenship required baptism and church attendance—not because they took their faith seriously.

What is forgotten in the allegation that Pietism is too otherworldly is the historical context. The Thirty Years' War was devastating and cost the German people much. The extent to which they lost is largely inestimable, but what can be calculated is this: three quarters of the total population were annihilated, the economy was virtually destroyed, and shame had descended on a people who endured what many historians have deemed a meaningless war fueled by religious struggles.[1] It is no surprise that hope—including any connection of the earthly with the heavenly—was severely lacking in a climate that revealed a church marked more by the spilled blood of division than the flowing waters of unity. Finding a haven in the other-worldly certainly would have been expected. Nevertheless, we must remember that the Pietists were the ones living in hope in this context. Accusations that their hope did not attend to this life are simply misguided. The Pietists were quite concerned for life on earth. They sought to renew the church, as we saw in Spener's program for revitalizing the church. They strove to change their social conditions, as we saw in Petersen's exercise of her gifts and Francke's reforms in Glaucha and Halle. Because they were people who enacted faith in love, they were able to imagine new life. All in all,

---

1. English historian C. V. Wedgwood is a prime example of one who called the Thirty Years' War "The futile and meaningless war." German socialist Gustav Freytag would be another. For more, see Rabb, *Thirty Years' War.*

Pietist hope is a particularly remarkable virtue among them, and they exuded it abundantly.

The way the Pietists practiced the virtue of hope has a lesson for Evangelicals: when it seems as though life is uninspiring or overwhelming, politics are not getting us anywhere, or the church seems more defined by sin than grace, don't despair. On the flip side, let your imaginations of the heavenly transform the earthly and shape who you become. As we said in chapter 4, people who hope build. People who hope also paint, as did Spener. Spener's hopeful proposals for a renewed church gave color to a world grayed by the aftermath of war. His six proposals were simple; nevertheless they communicated the "New Jerusalem" to the Christian church. By reimagining the church in a world of violence and destruction, Spener painted the church in contours of the gospel. He knew his church enough to know what it needed—hope. He knew his Bible enough to know what could be offered—a template for Christian living. Jesus's own vision for ministry along with Paul's letters to the Christian churches shaped the vision of what the church ought to become. The lesson for Evangelicals is not to despair. As our imaginations become more deeply formed by the Word, let it build and paint a vision of the people God desires us to be.

Angels or Worms? The Convergences in Pietist Christian Ethics

As I mentioned in chapter 1, Pietists liked to converge aspects of Christianity—doctrine and life, faith and social reform, word and deed. Their approach to Christian ethics was no different. While the Galatian motto of *faith active in love* is widely used to sum up Pietist ethics, we would be remiss if we did not acknowledge the inalterable convergence of the three traditional theological virtues as they make up the lifeblood of Pietist Christian ethics. The convergence of this triune set of God's gifts to humanity shaped their approach to individual piety, to ecclesial renewal, and social reform. And, within each of those spheres, reading Scripture was the principle habit that cultivated and fed each of the three excellences.

When we take seriously the living testimonies of the early figures of Philipp Jakob Spener, Johanna Eleonora Petersen, and August Hermann Francke, we see an embodied Christian ethic that transformed the church and world around them in ways far beyond following a set of principles or list of rules for faithful living. The moral life is more than a set of good practices, beliefs, or decisions. The moral life is also about Christian character. Moral formation is driven by who we are, who we ought to become, and how we ought to get there. Christian ethics asks such questions as, How should we believe?, How should we live?, and How should we hope?, because these questions lead us to engage the content of our faith, the holistic manner of love, and the gospel vision of hope. Christian morality is concerned with forming Christian character because a constellation of habits and actions are richer when they emerge from holistic Christians and connected with an integrated community of faith.

Character and action are one in the Pietist Christian ethic, and while this idea is not formally articulated in their writings, their ethic is evident in their biographical witnesses. The primary avenue that Christian character and corresponding actions converge in Pietism is evident in the ways they responded to the constellation of God's gifts to humanity—a constellation centered on the three primary virtues of faith, love, and hope. It is interesting to note that all of the three theological virtues are virtues whose noun forms and verbal forms converge, as I explain below. This is not the case for other virtues such as the four cardinal virtues of justice, courage, prudence, and temperance. In the former three, the excellence of character converges with the habit or action.

The Pietist ethic of convergence is such: we have faith, or belief (*pistis*), and we believe (*pisteuō*). When we receive faith, we "faith" by trusting and believing in God. We also receive content, namely God who is the content of our faith. In this way, both the knowledge of God and the act of trusting God converge as gift and response. We also have love (*agapē*) and we love (*agapaō*). We receive the capacity to love in God first loving us. We love by loving God in return and our neighbors as ourselves. In this way, both love of God and the act of loving our neighbor, converge as gift and response. Finally, we have hope (*elpis*) and we hope (*elpizō*). We receive hope through the vision of Jesus' ministry on earth—a ministry that ushered in the kingdom of God. We hope by living in the present with an eye on this promised kingdom. In this way, the now and the not-yet converge as gift and response.

Pietists converge. They are both angels and worms, and they both accept and overcome bogeys. They keep the lofty and the lowly in context and conversation with one another. Because they allowed God's Word in Scripture to penetrate their lives so deeply, things came together. In these convergences, the excellences, or virtues, are distinct from other virtues that we habituate in ourselves, because the theological virtues—faith, love, and hope—are first and foremost gifts received. The mechanics of convergence in Pietist Christian ethics has one last lesson for Evangelicals: gift and response are the heart of the gospel. The mechanics that bind us to God also bind us to one another. If we truly believe what Jesus preached, then we will receive one another and engage in the difficult, lifelong work of cultivating one another as the gifts they are, remembering that we are a common priesthood of angels and worms.

THE STORY GOES ON . . .

In 1740, St. George's church burned to the ground. So much was lost in the fire—from the foundation of the building to the pulpit to the art on the walls. Francke had been dead for over a decade, and though the church was still growing, the fire took its toll. The flaming rampage spared nothing—well, almost nothing. In the Francke Museum stands the only surviving relic of the fire—a communion chalice. Older than St. George's church itself, this chalice was the communion cup from which poor and wealthy, old and young, pastors and parishioners alike had received the blood of Christ, shed for all. The one simple thing the devastating fire spared was the cup of salvation, the hope of a people who would rebuild St. George's church in five short years.

My prayer to God for the church today is this: "Unite us in faith, encourage us with hope, and inspire us to love." This powerful communion prayer reminds us of three reasons that we come together as a common priesthood—to be united in faith, to be encouraged with hope, and to be inspired to love! We use the passive voice as it embodies what we believe to be true about human efforts in the face of our God and Creator, namely that faith, love, and hope are bestowed upon us by an act of grace. *We* do not achieve them, create them, or even merit them. When I think about the legacy that Pietism has left us, I immediately go to the communion chalice, around which Christians throughout time have gathered to receive and enact the Good News: Christ has died! Christ is Risen! Christ will come again! Amen.

Epilogue:
A Word to the Evangelical Covenant Church

The inspiration for this book was largely my own denomination, The Evangelical Covenant Church (ECC or Covenant). To those brothers and sisters, I write in hope that we might continue to remember our roots and journey together into the future embracing the gifts that Pietism has given us. There are many ways that Pietism has formed the Covenant. In everything from its constitution to its affirmations, its worship life and its attention to compassion, mercy, and justice, one can note seeds of Pietism germinating in the church today. As our preamble notes, Pietism forms the backbone of our theology and character.

> In continuity with the renewal movements of historic Pietism, the Evangelical Covenant Church especially cherishes the dual emphasis on new birth and new life in Christ, believing that personal faith in Jesus Christ as Savior and Lord is the foundation for our mission of evangelism and Christian nurture. Our common experience of God's grace and love in Jesus Christ continues to sustain the Evangelical Covenant Church as an interdependent

body of believers that recognizes but transcends
our theological differences.[1]

In addition, we are a church who has central affirmations
that shape the way we do theology, live into our identity as
Christians, and engage the church's mission. These affirmations begin with the Centrality of the Word of God and
include the Necessity of New Birth, A Commitment to the
Whole Mission of the Church, The Church as a Fellowship
of Believers, A Conscious Dependence on the Holy Spirit,
and The Reality of Freedom in Christ. Each of these six affirmations is embedded in Pietist commitments to a deep and
rooted faith, a transforming and charitable love, and a gospel-
shaped hope.

In reflecting on the ways that Pietism has and contin-
ues to influence the Covenant, I conducted two interviews.
The first was with C. John Weborg, Professor Emeritus of
Theology at North Park Theological Seminary.[2] Second, I in-
terviewed the current President of the Evangelical Covenant
Church, Gary B. Walter.[3]

Michelle: What are a couple of ways you think Pietism has
informed the ECC historically?

John: The Evangelical Covenant is an ecclesial piety who
has traditionally valued some of the gifts passed on by the
historical church, including confirmation, the lectionary, good preaching, and hymnody. One of the fruits of
this churchly Pietism is that while we treasure a personal

---

1. The Evangelical Covenant Church, "The Constitution and Bylaws
of the Evangelical Covenant Church," 1.

2. Weborg, Interview held on November 10, 2009.

3. Walter, interview held on November 11, 2009.

relationship with God, especially as summed up in the metaphor of God as friend in our hymnody, we do not take this relationship as private or individualistic. Our relationship with God is also a relationship with our brothers and sisters in Christ. When we affirm the church as the fellowship of believers, this comes from our ecclesial piety and is marked by the fruit of the Spirit. The fruit of the Spirit, furthermore, is a communal virtue that, when embodied, witnesses to the good news of Jesus Christ.

Michelle: How have our Pietist roots influenced the ECC as an evangelical church?

John: The sum total of congregational life at its best and most convincing is the body of Christ as a social apologetic for the gospel. This was abundantly clear in Spener, who, in the *Pia Desideria*, sought ways for the rebirth of congregational life in Germany. One of his points was that congregations are called to be compelling witness of the gospel, and that church accomplished its ministry when it empowered the common priesthood.

Michelle: Is there a word of challenge from Pietism for the ECC today?

John: The Pietist theme of the fear of God in relation to the radical gift of grace. Fear, for them, was never about terror of God's wrath or punishment; rather, it was the fear of *not* grasping the gift of God's free grace as a precious gift. Both German and Swedish Pietists were well aware that Luther's doctrine of justification could be taken advantage of, rather than understood as a radical statement of grace to be lived out by the church. The commitment to piety and Holy living was based on receiving this gift with a joyous thanksgiving. As John Newton's hymn "Amazing Grace" notes, grace teaches our hearts to fear and grace our fears relieve. We would do well to recover both fear and proper thankfulness in our worship and in our living.

Michelle: Where do you see the most exciting fruits of Pietism in the ECC?

John: In our mission. Our sense of the church's mission, both locally and abroad, is based on Francke and his missionary activities.

Michelle: Our most recent affirmation, "A Commitment to the Whole Mission of the Church," chronicles this ongoing development which began as a community of "Mission Friends." Do you see the influence of Pietism in the addition of the department of Compassion, Mercy, and Justice, as well as our ongoing outreach ministries around the world and World Missions?

John: Yes, that's right.

My second interview was with our president, Gary Walter, who responded as follows.

Michelle: What are a couple of ways you think Pietism has most gifted the Evangelical Covenant?

Gary: I believe our Pietistic heritage is intrinsic, and indispensible, to our identity. Often I hear people newer to the ECC (clergy and laity alike) say "I've been Covenant all along—I just didn't know it." I think what they are really saying is "I've been a Pietist all along—I just didn't know it." What resonates with people is the devotional approach to an orthodox faith more than the orthodoxy alone.

Michelle: What are one or two ways you think Pietism continues to influence the ECC? Are there any recent areas of growth or change that you would attribute to our Pietist heritage?

Gary: Pietism has given rise to our core ethos and character. Our ethos is derived from the interplay of four historic commitments. We are first a Biblical people. But knowing about God is not enough. Pietism directs us to the deeply personal knowing of God that those Scriptures reveal. And so we are also a devotional people. But even knowing God is not enough. Those Scriptures also call us to join God in God's work in the world to the lost and the hurting. And so we are thirdly a missional people. And finally, in meeting together in homes to study those Scriptures we understood that living with God and for God is much more powerful when lived out with others. We are a connectional people. Those four principles of being biblical, devotional, missional, and connectional all arise from a Pietistic approach to faith that still shape our distinctive identity today.

[Moreover], Pietism uniquely results in both humility and graciousness. If we are serious about internalizing the Word of God, we can do no other than live in gratefulness to God's goodness and grace. That's the source of humility. Knowing God wants to do the same for others leads to a graciousness of spirit, inviting others to experience what we ourselves have experienced.

Michelle: How does our rootedness in Pietism uniquely position us as an evangelical church?

Gary: At our most elemental, we are missional Pietists. We are Pietists who came together to form a mission society to do the work of Christ in the world. That means there is a simple rhythm to our identity: we live with God (our Pietistic side) and for God (our missional impulse). We want to move in two directions at the same time: deeper in Christ and further in mission. We pursue Christ and Christ's priorities in the world.

Michelle: Do you have any concluding thoughts on Pietism and the ECC? How does Pietism challenge the ECC today?

Gary: Deep in my heart I believe that there is a convergence between who we are and the yearnings of the day. Our core pietistic ethos and approach to mission and ministry is what can reach this world. We live in an increasingly post-Christian, post-modern, multiethnic environment. As such, people are hungering for a faith of authenticity, not plasticity; biblical depth and spirituality, not simply practicality; community, not individuality. They seek a faith that integrates kingdom values present and future, not simply looking to our eternal hope; of life-giving service to others, not self-interest; one that breaks down [all kinds of] barriers. That is precisely who we are at our best. Make no mistake. Who we are underlies our momentum as much as what we do.

Both Weborg and Walter affirm the depths to be celebrated and the gifts to be tapped in Pietism. Who we are, what we do, who we become, how we are the light of Christ in the world—all of these are ethical questions that we take up in conversation with past and present. All shape the way we communicate the good news, which marks the end toward which all Christian ethics aim. The words of our present church leaders are reminiscent of the late Covenant ethicist, Burton Nelson. In the foreword to *God's Glory, Neighbor's Good*, he wrote that the church's Pietist roots offer a perennial challenge for followers of Jesus Christ to bring together the glory of God and the good of the neighbor in everyday life.[4] "Gods glory, neighbor's good" has become one of the slogans of the Evangelical Covenant Church. It indicates the simple message that love of God and love of neighbor go hand in hand as the embodiment of the gospel of Jesus Christ. The Covenant cherishes this faithful, charitable, and irenic spirit, and such a posture is arguably a primary reason that the ECC continues to grow and flourish as a church. And so, to our Pietist mothers and fathers who entreat us to enact faith in love, for the glory of God and the good of our neighbor, we give thanks.

4. Sattler, *God's Glory, Neighbor's Good*, vii.

Bibliography

Augustine. *The Confessions of Saint Augustine*. Translated by John K. Ryan. Garden City, NY: Image, 1960.

Beyreuther, Erich. *August Hermann Francke*. Marburg: Francke, 1956.

Brown, Dale W. "The Bogey of Pietism." *Covenant Quarterly* 25:1 (1967) 12–18.

———. *Understanding Pietism*. Rev. ed. Nappanee, IN: Evangel, 1996.

Forell, George Wolfgang. *Faith Active in Love: An Investigation of Luther's Social Ethics*. New York: American, 1954.

Francke, August Hermann. "The Duty to the Poor." In *God's Glory, Neighbor's Good: A Brief Introduction to the Life and Writings of August Hermann Francke*, edited by Gary R. Sattler, 155–86. Chicago: Covenant, 1982.

———. "From the Autobiography." In *The Pietists: Selected Writings*, edited by Peter C. Erb, 99–216. New Jersey: Paulist, 1983.

Gawthrop, Richard L. *Pietism and the Making of Eighteenth-Century Prussia*. Cambridge: Cambridge University Press, 1993.

Herzog, Frederick. *European Pietism Reviewed*. San Jose: Pickwick, 2003.

Johnson, Todd E. "A Pietist Theology of Worship." *Covenant Quarterly* 58:4 (2000) 3–19.

Jung, Martin H. "Johanna Eleonora Petersen." In *The Pietist Theologians: An Introduction to the Theology in the Seventeenth and Eighteenth Centuries*, edited by Carter Lindberg. Oxford: Blackwell, 2005.

Martin, Lucinda. "Female Reformers as the Gatekeepers of Pietism: The Example of Johanna Eleonora Merlau and William Penn." *Monatshefte* 95 (2003) 34.

Moltmann, Jürgen. "Reformation and Revolution." In *Martin Luther and the Modern Mind: Freedom, Conscience, Toleration, Rights*, edited by Manfred Hoffmann, 163–90. Toronto Studies in Theology 22. Lewiston: Mellen, 1985.

Petersen, Johanna Eleonora. *The Life of Lady Johanna Eleonora Petersen, Written by Herself.* Edited and Translated by Barbara Becker-Cantarino. The Other Voice in Early Modern Europe. Chicago: University of Chicago Press, 2005.

———. "The Nature and Necessity of the New Creature in Christ." In *The Life of Lady Johanna Eleonora Petersen, Written by Herself,* edited by Barbara Becker-Cantarino. Translated by Francis Oakley. Chicago: University of Chicago Press, 2005.

Raabe, Paul. *A Guided Walk through the Francke Foundations.* Halle: Verlag der Franckeschen Stiftungen, 2003.

Rabb, Theodore K., editor. *The Thirty Years' War.* 2nd ed. Washington, DC: University Press of America, 1981.

Ritschl, Albrecht. *Geschichte des Pietismus in der lutherischen Kirche des 17 und 18 Jahrhunderts.* 2 vols. Bonn: Markus, 1884.

Sattler, Gary. *God's Glory, Neighbor's Good: A Brief Introduction to the Life and Writings of August Hermann Francke.* Chicago: Covenant, 1982.

———. *Nobler than the Angels, Lower than a Worm: The Pietist View of the Individual in the Writings of Heinrich Müller and August Hermannn Francke.* New York: University Press of America, 1989.

Schneider, Hans. *German Radical Pietism.* Translated by Gerald T. MacDonald. Toronto: Scarecrow, 2007.

Spener, Philipp Jakob. *Pia Desideria.* Translated by Theodore G. Tappert. Philadelphia: Fortress, 1964.

———. *The Spiritual Priesthood.* Translated by A. G. Voigt. Philadelphia: Lutheran, 1917.

Stein, K. James. *Philipp Jakob Spener: Pietist Patriarch.* Chicago: Covenant, 1986.

Stoeffler, F. Ernst. *The Rise of Evangelical Pietism.* Matrix: Studies in the History of Religions 9. Leiden: Brill, 1971.

Strom, Jonathan, Hartmut Lehmann, and James Van Horn Melton, editors. *Pietism in Germany and North America 1680–1820.* Burlington, VT: Ashgate, 2009.

Tolkien, J. R. R. *The Fellowship of the Ring.* New York: Quality Paperback Book Club, 2001.

Troeltsch, Ernst. *The Social Teachings of the Christian Churches.* Translated by Olive Wyon. New York: Harper, 1960.

Vogt, Peter. "In Search of the Invisible Church: The Role of Autobiographical Discourse in Eighteenth Century German Pietism." In *Confessionalism and Pietism: Religious Reform in Early Modern*

Europe, edited by Fred Van Lieburg, 293–312. Mainz: Von Zabern, 2006.

Walter, Gary B. Interview held on November 11, 2009.

Weborg, C. John. *The Eschatological Ethics of Johann Albrecht Bengel: Personal and Ecclesial Piety and the Literature of Edification in the Letters to the Seven Churches in Revelation 2 and 3*. Ann Arbor: University Microfilms International, 1983.

———. Interview held on November 10, 2009.

———. "Pietism: A Question of Meaning and Vocation." *Covenant Quarterly* 41:3 (1983) 59–71.

Weisner, Mary. *Gender, Church, and State in Early Modern Germany*. London: Longman, 1998.

Yoder, John Howard. *Christian Witness to the State*. Newton, KS: Faith and Life, 1964.

———. *The Politics of Jesus: Vicit Agnus Noster*. Grand Rapids: Eerdmans, 1972.